# NIGHT OF THE
# PUPPET PEOPLE

NIGHT OF THE LIVING DUMMY
DEEP TROUBLE
MONSTER BLOOD
THE HAUNTED MASK
ONE DAY AT HORRORLAND
THE CURSE OF THE MUMMY'S TOMB
BE CAREFUL WHAT YOU WISH FOR
SAY CHEESE AND DIE!
THE HORROR AT CAMP JELLYJAM
HOW I GOT MY SHRUNKEN HEAD
THE WEREWOLF OF FEVER SWAMP
A NIGHT IN TERROR TOWER
WELCOME TO DEAD HOUSE
WELCOME TO CAMP NIGHTMARE
GHOST BEACH
THE SCARECROW WALKS AT MIDNIGHT
YOU CAN'T SCARE ME!
RETURN OF THE MUMMY
REVENGE OF THE LAWN GNOMES
PHANTOM OF THE AUDITORIUM
VAMPIRE BREATH
STAY OUT OF THE BASEMENT
A SHOCKER ON SHOCK STREET
LET'S GET INVISIBLE!
NIGHT OF THE LIVING DUMMY 2
NIGHT OF THE LIVING DUMMY 3
THE ABOMINABLE SNOWMAN OF PASADENA
THE BLOB THAT ATE EVERYONE
THE GHOST NEXT DOOR
THE HAUNTED CAR
ATTACK OF THE GRAVEYARD GHOULS
PLEASE DON'T FEED THE VAMPIRE

## ALSO AVAILABLE:
IT CAME FROM OHIO!: MY LIFE AS A WRITER by R.L. Stine

## NIGHT OF THE
## PUPPET PEOPLE

# R.L. STINE

SCHOLASTIC INC.

Goosebumps book series created by Parachute Press, Inc.
Copyright © 2015 by Scholastic Inc.

ISBN 978-0-545-62775-7

12  11  10  9  8  7  6                    16  17  18  19/0

Printed in the U.S.A.                                        40
First printing, October 2015

# WELCOME. YOU ARE MOST WANTED.

Come in. I'm R.L. Stine. Welcome to the Goosebumps office.

Sorry about the smell. I was making my famous Stinkweed Pancakes for breakfast. It's very hard to find stinkweed that smells good these days. But it's delicious if you hold your nose when you swallow.

Care for some breakfast? How about a bowl of cereal? Let's see . . . I have Mice Krispies. And here's a box of Bunny Nut Cheerios. Don't you love that cereal? The way the furry little pieces of bunny get stuck in your teeth?

You're not hungry? How about a slice of this nice green melon? Oh, wait. Sorry. That's not a melon. It's the shrunken head I got this week.

Ha-ha. Look. I took a bite out of it before I realized what it was.

Whoa. You're starting to look as green as this shrunken head.

I see you're admiring the WANTED posters on the wall. Those posters show the creepiest, crawliest, grossest Goosebumps characters of all time. They are the MOST WANTED CHARACTERS from the MOST WANTED books.

That poster you are studying has two weird-looking puppets on it. I hate it when puppets look so lifelike — don't you? They look like real people — Puppet People!

Ben and Jenny Renfro can tell you a story about these puppets, a story about puppets so frightening, you'll wonder who is pulling the strings.

Go ahead. Read their story. Find out why the Puppet People are MOST WANTED.

# PROLOGUE

# SEVEN YEARS AGO

# 1

"Jenny, don't fight with your brother. It's your birthday," Mrs. Renfro said.

"But he took the candy bar I wanted!" Jenny cried.

"Did not!" Ben squeezed the miniature Snickers bar in his fist. He made his mean face at Jenny.

Mrs. Renfro sighed. She blew a strand of blond hair off her forehead. "Why don't you two share it? You're twins. You should share *everything*."

"Ben never shares anything," Jenny pouted. She made a wild swipe for the candy in her brother's hand. But he snatched it away from her. "Get your own, Stink Head."

"Ben, don't call names on your birthday. You're five now. You have to act more like a gentleman."

"No, I don't," Ben insisted. "I don't even know what that means."

Mrs. Renfro had to laugh. She brushed a hand through Ben's curly brown hair. Ben was stubborn, but he knew how to make her laugh.

"Mom, don't laugh. He isn't funny," Jenny said.

Jenny loved scolding her mother. And she seldom let Ben bully her. Even though they were twins and looked alike, Jenny was already an inch taller than her brother.

Mrs. Renfro heard a shout and turned to the sound. All around the living room, the five-year-old party guests were smearing chocolate on their cheeks and chins. *I guess the little candy bars were a bad idea*, Mrs. Renfro thought. *I should have bought M&M's.*

She pushed her way through the room. "What was the shouting about?" she asked.

Anna Richards, in a frilly pink party dress, pointed to the chubby boy with short black hair at the coffee table. "Jonathan spilled his apple juice," she reported. "He's a klutz."

Mrs. Renfro squinted at her. "Anna, where did you learn that word?"

"From *Sesame Street.*"

Jonathan Sparrow lived across the street. He and Ben and Jenny had playdates all the time. Now he was staring at a dark, wet spot on the front of his denim overalls.

"Don't worry about it," Mrs. Renfro said. "It'll dry."

"I spilled on the table, too," Jonathan said, avoiding her eyes.

She hurried to the kitchen to get paper towels. On her way back to the living room, the man with the long white beard stopped her. He wore a silky purple robe that came down to the floor. A tall, pointed red cap. And he had a long purple scarf wrapped around his neck.

"Is it time for the show?" he asked.

Mrs. Renfro nodded. "Good idea. Before it gets *really* messy in here!"

"Five-year-olds love chocolate," he said, scratching his beard.

She sighed. "I never should have given it to them." She waved the paper towels. "First, let me mop up a spill. Then we'll get started."

She hurried back to the living room. She glimpsed Jenny sitting cross-legged on the floor. Jenny had *three* candy bars in her lap. She always found a way to beat Ben.

Where was Ben? Wrestling on the rug with a red-haired boy from his kindergarten class.

"Let's all sit on the floor! Hurry!" she shouted. "Everyone sit down and face the fireplace. We have a surprise for you."

They were excited about the surprise, but it still took ten minutes to get them all seated. "Quiet, everyone!" Mrs. Renfro said. "Be very quiet. You don't want to miss the fun."

7

Ben and Jenny couldn't wait to find out what the surprise was. Mrs. Renfro smiled at their eager faces.

*What a great idea it was to have this show,* she thought.

Mrs. Renfro didn't know the horror was about to begin.

The man with the full white beard stepped quickly to the front of the room, swirling his long purple robe. "I am Wizzbang the Wizard!" he declared. His shout startled Ben, who bounced on the floor beside his sister.

"I have some magic to show you!" the wizard shouted. "Does anyone want to see some magic?"

The kids obediently cried yes.

Ben squinted at the wizard, who moved rapidly from side to side, his robe swishing over the rug. What was that in his long beard? A black spot that appeared to be moving.

Was that a spider in his beard?

Ben shivered. He didn't like spiders. Once, a spider got into his bed and crawled under his pajama shirt while he was just falling asleep. It didn't bite him, but Ben felt itchy every time he thought about spiders.

"Here comes the magic!" Wizzbang exclaimed. "Watch carefully, everyone."

Ben forced himself to look away from the black spot in the wizard's beard. He reached over Jenny and punched Jonathan on the shoulder.

"Shhh." Jonathan raised a finger to his lips. "I'm watching."

Wizzbang reached a hand into his robe and pulled out a tall marionette. She had a sparkly tiara on her head and was dressed in a long blue ball gown. It took Wizzbang a few seconds to get her strings untangled. They were attached to crisscrossed wooden control sticks. He sorted them out and made her stand up straight.

"This is the princess!" he announced. He leaned over the puppet. His long beard brushed the top of her tiara. Using both hands on the sticks, he made her take a few steps toward the audience.

"The princess is not a puppet. She is a marionette. But when Wizzbang the Wizard pulls her strings, she comes alive."

Ben stared at the princess as Wizzbang made her do a graceful dance. "She's almost as tall as we are," Jenny said.

"So what?" Ben replied. Jonathan laughed.

"Be quiet," Jenny snapped.

Ben watched the puppet dip and glide. Her eyes looked like real people eyes. Her lips were painted in a pale red smile. Beneath the tiara, her straight blond hair looked real, too.

Wizzbang pulled a string and made her raise one hand above her head. Then he moved the string, and her hand bobbed up and down as if she were waving to the kids.

"The princess has come from far away to wish happy birthday to Ben and Jenny," the wizard said. He made the marionette walk up to Ben. Her glassy eyes appeared to gaze down at him.

Ben raised himself to his knees. He took the puppet's small hand and pretended to shake hands with her.

Some kids laughed. But not for long.

The princess dipped suddenly. Her head dropped. Her mouth opened. And her wooden jaw clamped tight over Ben's shoulder.

He let out a cry of pain.

He tried to shake the puppet off. But her jaw tightened even harder, biting into his skin.

"It HURTS!" Ben screamed at Wizzbang. "Take her OFF me! It hurts. It REALLY hurts!"

Wizzbang's mouth dropped open. "I — I — don't understand," he stammered.

He let go of the strings and wrapped both hands around the puppet's head. After a short struggle, he pulled the puppet off Ben.

"It ... really ... hurts ..." Ben murmured. He was trying hard not to cry. He didn't want to cry on his birthday in front of all the kids. He rubbed his shoulder, but the pain kept shooting down his whole body.

"What happened?" Ben heard his mother ask. She was standing behind the kids, at the doorway to the dining room.

"The strings must have gotten tangled up," Wizzbang said. "And the mouth got stuck. Sorry, Ben." He rubbed Ben's shoulder. "Not to worry. I have another puppet."

He returned a few seconds later with a new puppet. This one had a crown on his head and wore a flashy leopard-skin robe.

"Say hello to the sultan," Wizzbang said. "He's the king."

Ben was still rubbing his shoulder. He heard a few kids talking about the puppet that bit him. They sounded scared.

"Ben, I'm sorry about the princess," the wizard said. "It was a bad accident. But you're okay, right?"

Ben nodded and muttered yes under his breath.

"These puppets are really fun to operate," Wizzbang said. "Would anyone like to stand up and work the sultan?"

No one raised a hand. The room grew very silent.

"It's very simple," Wizzbang said. "You pull the strings. Just like this." He made the sultan bow. Then he pulled some strings and the puppet's hands shot up in the air.

"Who would like to try it?" the wizard asked. "Jenny? You're the birthday girl. Come up here and meet the sultan."

Jenny climbed to her feet slowly. She glanced at Ben, then stepped up to the front of the room.

"Come closer," Wizzbang said. "Why are you standing so far away?"

Jenny frowned at the puppet. "Does he bite?"

"No. Of course not," the wizard answered. "Here, Jenny. Take the controls." He handed her the control sticks.

"He's heavy!" Jenny exclaimed.

"These marionettes are large and very tall," the wizard said. "And they are made of heavy wood. Go ahead. Make him walk."

Jenny balanced the control sticks in her hands. She lowered one set of strings, and the sultan bowed. She made him stand up straight again. Then she made him raise one hand in the air.

The hand shot straight up — and grabbed Jenny by the nose.

Jenny let out a startled scream.

She felt the wooden fingers tighten. Her nose throbbed with pain. And the pain quickly spread over her face and down her neck.

"Owwwww!" Jenny's cry rang out through the room. "STOP it!"

The puppet squeezed hard, squeezed Jenny's nose till she thought her nose might burst apart!

Wizzbang appeared to freeze. He stared wide-eyed at the puppet.

Kids started to cry. Some of them jumped to their feet and backed out of the room.

The strings fell out of Jenny's hands and piled on the floor. Jenny squirmed and twisted, trying to get free. She dropped to her knees, wailing in pain.

Now a lot of kids were crying. Jenny saw her mother rushing toward her, her mouth open in shock, eyes bulging.

"So sorry. So sorry," Wizzbang finally found his voice. Behind his white beard, his face was bright red. Jenny saw big drops of sweat rolling down his forehead. "So sorry. So sorry."

With a hard tug, he managed to pull the sultan's fingers off Jenny's nose. Her nose throbbed with pain.

"That's going to leave a nasty bruise," Jenny's mom said. She put her arms around Jenny and hugged her tight.

"So sorry," the wizard repeated. It was hard to hear him over the shrieks and wails of the crying kids.

He swept his puppets over his arm, shaking his head, apologizing again and again. "I don't know what happened. I can't explain it. I'm so, sooo sorry."

Tripping over dangling marionette strings, he stumbled to the front door. He darted out of the house and vanished. He didn't even bother to shut the door behind him.

Jenny wiped tears from her eyes. She saw her dad burst into the room, staring at all the crying kids. "What happened?" he asked her mom.

Mrs. Renfro shrugged. "I'm not sure."

Ben stepped over to them. His face was very pale and he was shaking, hands stuffed in his pockets. "Those puppets were bad," he said. "Very bad."

# PART ONE

# SEVEN YEARS LATER

# 4

Whenever my twin sister, Jenny, and I run into Anna Richards and her BFF, Maria Salinas, we try to be nice. I mean, we're in sixth grade and we've known them since kindergarten. We'd like to be friends with those two — but they're impossible.

Take today, for instance. It was three o'clock, and Jenny and I were making our way through the crush of kids leaving Ringler Middle School. Something fell out of my backpack. I dropped down to pick it up, and when I stood up, there were Anna and Maria.

They always have these sneers on their faces. They're not smiling. They're saying: *We know something you don't.* Or maybe: *We're so much better than you, it makes us smile like this.*

"Clumsy much?" Anna said to me. Her green eyes flashed, like maybe she had just made a funny joke.

Maria laughed. She laughs at everything her

friend Anna says. Maria is very pretty. She has big, dark eyes and wavy black hair like a waterfall halfway down her back.

"I like your vest," Jenny said to Anna. My sister, Jenny, is a very friendly person. I mean, everyone likes Jenny. And she's always trying to be friendly to Anna and Maria.

But why bother?

"You have good taste," Anna replied, running her hand along one side of the vest. "I don't think it would look good on you. It would clash with your pimples."

"I don't have pimples," Jenny protested. "Those are freckles!"

"Ben, I hear you had a major fail on the algebra test," Maria said. And there went that smug sneer again.

"Algebra and I don't get along," I murmured. "Mr. Deacon said I could take it again. I know I'll do better the second time."

"Well, you couldn't do any *worse*, could you?" Maria said. She laughed a big, cruel laugh.

Suddenly, Jenny lost it. "Don't you ever get tired of being mean?" she snapped at Maria.

Maria didn't blink. "No," she replied.

She and Anna bumped knuckles.

Like, *Aren't we awesome.*

Anna pulled a sheet of paper from her backpack and held it up to me. "This is what an A on the test looks like."

I rolled my eyes. "You're too kind."

Of course, I knew Anna and Maria got A's on the test. They get A's in everything. They are always at the top of the school honor roll. And they win every essay contest and every trophy and every spelling bee and everything that anyone can win.

They are the best at everything. Just ask them.

Anna tucked her perfect A test back into her backpack. "Tell me," she said, "what are you doing for the Sixth-Grade Variety Show? Making rude noises?"

Maria laughed.

I shrugged. "Beats me. We don't know what to do."

"There's a five-hundred-dollar prize," Maria said. "Anna and I are trying to decide what to do with all that money when we win."

"You could donate it to the BRF," I said.

Anna sneered at me. "What's that?"

"It's the Ben Renfro Fund. It's a charity I'm thinking of starting," I told her.

"You're so hilarious," Anna said without cracking a smile.

"What are you two doing in the show?" Jenny asked.

"A puppet skit," Maria answered, tossing her long hair back over her shoulder.

"We made these awesome marionettes," Anna said. "And we've been taking puppeteer lessons at the Y. No one there can believe how good we are."

I stared at them without replying. I felt a chill roll down my back. It's a totally weird thing. I'm kind of afraid of puppets. Jenny is, too. We don't know why.

Jenny squeezed my arm. I knew she had the same strange feeling. "We might do a rap," she told them.

Anna rolled her eyes. "Very original."

"Like no one else would think of that," Maria added.

I could feel my face turning red. I wasn't blushing. I was *angry*. I really couldn't talk to Anna and Maria for more than five minutes. After that, I wanted to explode — or make *them* explode!

Finally, they let us go. Jenny and I walked out of the school building. I took deep breaths of the cool spring air. I always felt like it was hard to breathe around those two girls.

Jenny shook her head. "They're like one of those bad teen movies," she said. "You know. Where the mean girls rule the school."

"I sure would love to win that prize money," I said. "I could use some new video games. If I had five hundred dollars . . ."

"Forget about it," Jenny said. "Anna and Maria always win. It's a school rule."

I balled my hands into tight fists. "I'd do *anything* to beat them in this variety show," I said. "Seriously. I'd do *anything*."

Famous last words?

# 5

After dinner that night, Jenny and I went to our friend Jonathan Sparrow's house to talk about the variety show. Jonathan is tall, very skinny, and he has tiny, round black eyes over a bent nose that resembles a bird's beak. But that's not why everyone calls him Bird. Everyone calls him Bird because his last name is Sparrow.

Duh.

Jenny and I have known Bird our whole life, mainly because our parents are good friends, and we live across the street from one another. Tonight we had the house to ourselves. Bird's mother was away on a business trip. And his dad is coach of the high school soccer team, and he was at soccer practice.

Bird is kind of a tense guy. He likes to pace back and forth when he's thinking about something. And right now he was thinking about the variety show.

Jenny and I sat on opposite ends of the long

brown leather couch in the living room and watched Bird wear out the carpet with his pacing. Jenny was chewing on a PayDay bar, which she refused to share with me. "You might be allergic to peanuts," she said.

I groaned. "You know I'm not allergic to peanuts."

"It might be a new allergy you just got today," she said. "How can you be sure?"

"Let's forget about peanut allergies and talk about what we're going to do," Bird said. He wiped his hands on the sides of his jeans. He always has sweaty hands. He says it's a family trait.

"I think we have one big problem," he said. "We don't have any talent."

"Bird nailed it," Jenny said, swallowing the last chunk of the candy bar. "We can't sing. We can't dance. We don't play any instruments. We have no talent."

"Are we going to let a little thing like that stop us?" I said.

They both laughed. Jenny gave me a shove. "Since when are you the cheerful one? That's supposed to be my job."

"I'm not being cheerful. I just want to win the five hundred dollars."

"Hey. Do you know how to yodel?" Bird asked.

"No," Jenny and I said in unison.

"Neither do I," Bird said.

"Maybe we could do some kind of play," I said. "You know. A comedy skit."

"Are we funny?" Bird asked.

"You're both funny *looking*," Jenny said.

I swiped my hand over her head and messed up her hair.

Bird started to say something. But he stopped when we heard heavy footsteps in the hall. Coach Sparrow burst into the room. He tossed his soccer jersey onto a chair.

"Dad — you're home early," Bird said.

"Yeah. I stopped practice early because there's a big storm coming." He has a gruff voice that always sounds hoarse. He doesn't really look like a big jock soccer coach. He's tall and lanky like Bird, and he wears these square, black-framed glasses that make him look more like an English teacher.

"What are you guys doing?" he asked. He pulled the whistle from around his neck and tossed it onto his jersey.

"Schoolwork," Bird answered.

Coach Sparrow nodded. "I'm going to check all the windows. Hear that wind howling out there? The rain is on the way."

He trotted out of the room. Bird waited for him to move out of sight. Then he said, "I have an idea."

"Do we have to learn how to play violins?" I said.

25

Bird shook his head. "No. No violins. We have to go up to the attic, but my dad never wants me to go up there," he whispered.

"Why? Is it haunted?" Jenny demanded. She is the horror freak in the family. She always wants places to be haunted. I guess that means she's braver than me. But we don't have to get into that.

"I don't know why," Bird continued, whispering. "He never told me. But, listen. There are old clothes up there. Piles of them. They might make great costumes for a comedy skit."

"Awesome," Jenny said. "Let's go check them out." She jumped off the couch and pulled me to my feet.

"Wait," Bird ordered. He checked the back hallway and glanced around. "Okay. The coast is clear."

He led us to the attic door, in the hall past the kitchen. He pulled the door open and fumbled on the wall for a light switch. A dim orange light washed over the steep steps. "Okay. Follow me," he whispered.

I hung back. "Are you sure this is okay?"

"I guess we won't know till we get up there," Bird said.

# 6

As we started to climb, the wooden stairs groaned like we were hurting them. I gripped the slender banister. It trembled under my hand. It seemed about to fall off the wall.

The air in the stairwell was hot and damp. I could feel drops of sweat on the back of my neck. Above us, the storm winds howled, so loud I thought they were blowing through the house.

The orange ceiling light blinked. It glowed so dimly, I could barely make out my shoes on the stairs.

Bird led the way, followed by Jenny. They were nearly to the top of the stairs. I was still halfway down, trying to get my heartbeat to slow, telling myself there was nothing to be afraid of.

*It's just an attic filled with old junk.*

The wind gave a loud howl, and the orange light flickered again. The banister shook in my hand. Why did the air suddenly smell so sour?

Bird and Jenny reached the top. Their shoes clumped onto the attic floorboards. "Are you sure this attic isn't haunted?" Jenny asked.

I didn't hear Bird's answer.

I climbed the creaking stairs to the top. The attic was small, with stacks of cartons everywhere. A window rattled at one end. The ceiling came slanting down on both sides, barely a foot over our heads.

An old armchair was covered by a stained gray blanket. I saw a baby crib against the wall. The crib was filled with piles of old books.

"Spooky," Jenny said, gazing around.

"No, it isn't," Bird replied. "It's just a lot of my parents' old stuff."

"But it's spooky with the wind howling," I said. "And the flickering light. And the —"

I didn't get to finish what I was saying. Because something came flying across the long room. Not flying, exactly. It came *shooting* across the room, bumping the low ceiling as it darted closer.

*Straight for my head!*

A bat! A red-eyed bat, its wings flapping loudly.

I tried to duck out of its way. But I stumbled back into Jenny.

The bat screeched as it shot overhead. I could feel the wind off its wings in my hair.

Jenny and I both tumbled backward into a tall stack of cartons.

28

"Noooo!" A scream escaped my mouth as the cartons toppled over.

Jenny and I landed in sitting positions on the floor. With a groan, I pulled myself to my feet. Then I turned to look at the fallen cartons.

And then we saw what Bird's father had hidden back there.

# 7

A dark wooden cabinet. All three of us stared at it in surprise. It was tall and wide and had two doors across the front. It was covered by a thick layer of dust.

Bird stepped past Jenny and me to the front of the cabinet. Then he rubbed a finger along one door. "This dust is an inch thick. No one has touched this cabinet in a long time."

"Open it," Jenny said. "Let's see what's inside."

I stepped in front of Bird. "Maybe we shouldn't," I said. "I mean, maybe Bird's parents hid it back there for a reason."

"You mean because it's haunted?" Jenny said.

"Shut up," I snapped. "Stop talking about things being haunted."

Jenny laughed. "You are so brave, Ben." Then, of course, she added: "Not."

"I don't see *you* pulling the doors open," I said to Jenny. "Go ahead. Do it." I gave her a little shove toward the cabinet.

She stopped short. She took a step back.

"I think we should go back downstairs," Bird said. "My dad is always telling me the attic is dangerous. I told you, he never wants me to come up here."

"Bird, it was *your* idea," I said. "What's your problem?"

"I decided I don't like attics."

I stared hard at the cabinet doors. *I'll be the brave one for once*, I thought. "Let's just take a peek," I said.

I pushed Jenny out of the way and raised my hand to the door on the right. I gripped the round wooden knob and tugged.

*"Look out!"* Jenny screamed at the top of her lungs.

I uttered a cry and stumbled back.

Jenny laughed. "Only kidding."

"Not funny," I said. "You didn't scare me." At least they couldn't hear my heart pounding like a bass drum in my chest. "Not funny at all."

I grabbed the knobs on both doors and pulled. No. The doors wouldn't budge.

"Stuck," I said. "I need something to pry them open."

"Let's just leave it shut," Bird said. "Probably just old clothes in there anyway."

"Is that a tool kit?" Jenny asked. She pointed to a black metal box tucked against the wall.

I dropped to my knees and unlatched the lid.

Then I pulled a long screwdriver from inside. "This should work," I said.

"Ben, you know you're terrified," Jenny said. "Why are you doing this?"

"We'll see who's terrified," I said. I turned and dug the tip of the screwdriver into the crack between the door and the cabinet.

And as I did, a deafening explosion of thunder shook the house.

"Whoooa." A cry escaped my throat.

And the lights went out.

I blinked. We were standing there in total darkness.

None of us spoke. The howl of the wind sweeping across the roof was the only sound we heard.

I kept blinking, as if it would help me see better.

"Too bad we didn't bring a flashlight," Jenny said. Her voice cracked.

"Yeah. Too bad," Bird said. "I can't see a thing."

I heard a soft giggle. "Jenny? What's so funny?" I asked.

"It wasn't me," she said. "Did you laugh, Bird?"

"No way," he said.

I felt a chill at the back of my neck. And heard another soft laugh, just above a whisper.

"Come on, Jenny, you're not funny," I said. "Stop doing that."

"I *told* you, it wasn't me," she insisted.

"It sounded like it was coming from the cabinet," Bird said.

"No way," I replied.

I heard another soft giggle.

And then a cold hand grabbed me by the throat.

"Gaaaack." The cold hand closed around my throat. I started to gag. I jerked my whole body back, freeing myself from the icy grip. "Who did that?" I choked out in a weak, trembling voice. I could still feel the cold, hard fingers on my throat.

"Oh. Sorry," Jenny said. "Was that you? I didn't mean to scare you. Really."

"You did it on purpose!" I cried.

"No —" Jenny started. "I didn't. Really, I —" She stopped as a beam of gray-green light swept over the attic wall. Light from a flashlight.

"Is someone up there?" Coach Sparrow's voice from downstairs.

"Yeah, Dad. We're up here," Bird called down to him.

The wide circle of light moved back and forth over the ceiling and wall.

"Why are you up there? What are you doing?"

"Uh . . ." Bird hesitated. "We're just looking through old clothes for costumes."

"I don't like you being up there," his father shouted. "Especially in this storm."

Another roar of thunder made the attic shake. The window rattled against the howling winds.

"I'm tossing the flashlight up," Coach Sparrow said. It thudded onto the attic floor and rolled to the wall. The beam of light shone on our frightened faces. "Use it to come downstairs."

"Okay, Dad," Bird called. "Be right down."

"Maybe we could do a comedy skit about three kids trapped in the dark in a haunted attic," Jenny said.

"Stop saying *haunted*," I snapped. I realized I still had the screwdriver gripped tightly in my hand. "Hey, Bird, beam the light on the cabinet," I said.

"Dad wants us to go downstairs," Bird said.

"It'll only take a second," I replied. "Don't you want to know what's inside there?"

He swung the flashlight up and aimed the light at the wooden doors.

I plunged the screwdriver forward and struggled to pry open one of the doors. It didn't budge.

I gripped the screwdriver handle in both hands and pushed harder.

I nearly fell as both doors swung open. Then the attic rang with our screams as a man came leaping out at us.

9

He fell at my knees, his arms wrapped around my legs.

Bird dropped the flashlight. It clattered on the floor.

Jenny screamed again.

I froze. I couldn't move. Or make a sound.

By the time Bird picked up the flashlight and shone it in my direction, I realized it wasn't a man that had tumbled from the open cabinet.

I dropped down to examine it. A puppet. A tall marionette, the strings tangled around its body. One arm was draped limply around my leg.

I lifted it off the floor and held it up to Jenny and Bird. "It's a puppet," I said. I tried to untangle the strings. It was a girl puppet with long, straight blond hair and a tiara on her head.

"A princess puppet," Jenny said.

I felt my body shudder. I handed the puppet to Bird. I don't know why, but puppets have creeped me out ever since I was a kid. I get this heavy feeling in the pit of my stomach whenever I see a puppet. I know it's weird. But it happens.

Jenny isn't as bad as I am, but she feels weird around puppets, too. She can't explain it, either.

Bird handed me the flashlight. "Are there more in the cabinet?" he asked. He rested the princess puppet against the wall and stepped up to the cabinet. "Check it out." He pulled out a tall marionette with a shield and a sword attached.

"A knight to go with the princess," Jenny said.

"And one more," Bird said. He pulled out a puppet in a purple robe. This one had a black beard and wore a jeweled turban. "Must be a king," Bird said. "A sultan."

Jenny and I stared at the marionettes in Bird's hands. "Why do they look familiar?" Jenny asked.

I shrugged. "Beats me." I gazed down at the princess puppet, folded against the wall. "Bird, why did your parents hide them away up here?"

Bird shook his head. "Maybe they're valuable. You know. Maybe they're worth a ton of money, and my parents were afraid someone might steal them."

"Maybe . . ." I said.

"We can ask your dad," Jenny said.

Bird shook his head. "No. No way. He might get really steamed because we went into the cabinet. He might —"

"What's that on the bottom shelf?" Jenny asked, pointing.

37

I turned the flashlight back to the cabinet. Jenny reached down and pulled something out. At first, I thought it was a towel. But when I shone the light on it, I saw that it was a white beard. A long, fake beard.

"Ooh, creepy," Jenny said with a shudder. She shoved the beard back onto the bottom shelf.

"These puppets are awesome," Bird said, holding the knight and the sultan at his sides. "They make Anna and Maria's puppets look like baby toys."

"Huh?" I turned to him. "You saw their puppets?"

He nodded. "Yeah. They were practicing in the music room at school. Anna and Maria made the puppets themselves — and they look it. They're kind of like rag dolls with strings."

I studied the puppets. They didn't look amateur or homemade. For one thing, these were very tall, at least three feet tall. And they had awesome faces, not just paint on wood. The eyes were glassy and the eyelids blinked. Their costumes were well made and didn't look like doll clothes.

Another explosion of thunder rocked the house. Lightning crackled nearby, making the narrow room bright as day for a second or two.

In the strange light, I caught a thoughtful expression on Bird's face. "Uh-oh," I said. "What's going on in that little brain of yours?"

"I'm thinking about the puppets. Thinking about the variety show. Thinking maybe —"

"Don't say it," I said. "Stop thinking."

"Thinking maybe we could do a great skit with these puppets," Bird continued.

"No way!" Jenny and I cried at the same time.

"Jenny and I don't like puppets," I said. "We have a thing about puppets. The whole idea is giving me the creeps."

"Get over it," Bird said. "You want to win the five hundred dollars — don't you?"

"We can't do puppets," Jenny insisted. "How can we do puppets if Anna and Maria are already doing puppets?"

"Look at these puppets," Bird said. "They're awesome. They're a thousand times better than their babyish rag dolls. Our puppets can *kill* their puppets!"

That made Jenny and me laugh.

"Bird is right," I told Jenny. "Maybe we can finally beat them at something."

"But puppets give me nightmares," Jenny said, her eyes on the princess puppet. "You too, Ben."

"Maybe Bird is right about that, too," I said. "Maybe it's time to get over it."

"Let's see if we can figure out how to work these things," Bird said.

We propped the flashlight up so that it cast a broad beam of light over the ceiling. Then we each took a marionette. It took a while to untangle the strings.

They were attached to crisscrossing wooden

control sticks. One stick held the strings for the head and the hands. The foot and leg strings were attached to the other stick.

I had the sultan puppet. The strings were totally tangled in his long robe. Jenny was practicing with the princess puppet. She tilted the control sticks, and the puppet's head bobbed from side to side.

"These are way cool," Bird murmured. He made the knight puppet stagger across the floor. "But it's going to take a while to figure out which string does what."

I finally untangled the knots in the sultan's leg strings. I raised the control sticks till he stood up straight. The tiny jewels in the sultan's turban sparkled in the light cast down by the flashlight.

I still had a heavy feeling of dread in the pit of my stomach. But I was determined to get over my ridiculous fear. "Check this out," I said.

I moved the sultan forward across the floor. I made him swing his arms as his legs rose and fell. It looked as if he was walking!

I turned him around and then had him walk up to the princess. He raised a hand to his middle and took a low bow.

"Wow!" Bird exclaimed. "Ben, that's excellent. How did you do that?"

"I . . . I'm not sure," I stammered. "It was easy. It was almost like he was walking *himself.*"

# 10

We practiced for a few more minutes. Bird figured out how to make the knight marionette wave his sword in the air. Jenny quickly became good at making the princess glide gracefully over the floor, holding her head high like royalty.

Working the sultan seemed to come naturally to me. I really wasn't sure what I was doing. The puppet really did seem to move on its own.

"Are you still up there?" Coach Sparrow's shout echoed off the attic walls.

"Coming!" Bird called down to him.

We carefully hung the puppets back in the cabinet and made sure the doors were shut tight. Sheets of rain pounded the roof above us. The electricity was still off.

We used the flashlight to guide our way down the steep, creaking attic stairs. Coach Sparrow, a halogen lantern in one hand, greeted us in the hallway. "You guys were up there a long time," he said. "Did you find anything interesting?"

"Not really," Bird answered quickly.

His dad turned to Jenny and me. "I spoke to your mother. I told her since the storm is so bad, you two should sleep over here. And she agreed."

"Yaaay. A sleepover!" Bird declared, pumping his fists in the air. "Can we have hot chocolate and Oreos? Aren't you supposed to have hot chocolate and Oreos at a sleepover?"

Jenny rolled her eyes. "You've been watching the Disney Channel too much," she said.

"Anyway, we can't make hot chocolate without electricity," Bird said.

"We have a gas stove, remember?" Coach Sparrow said. "I think we can manage it."

He lit some candles in the kitchen, and we sat at the counter with our sleepover snacks. Jenny and I didn't have our usual argument over the best way to eat an Oreo. That's because we only wanted to talk about our puppet skit.

As soon as Bird's dad was out of the room, we started thinking up jokes and story ideas and talking about how Anna and Maria were going to be so shocked and horrified when they saw how much better our marionettes were.

Coach Sparrow returned to the kitchen to bring us more flashlights. And we immediately stopped the puppet talk and changed the subject to the storm. Bird really didn't want his dad to know we'd found the puppets. I guess Bird thought he'd say we couldn't use them, and then we wouldn't have anything at all for the variety show.

Lightning flashed outside Bird's bedroom windows. The thunder was so close, it sounded like it was coming from *inside* the house.

Bird has bunk beds in his room. I hoisted myself up to the top bunk, and he dropped into the bottom. Jenny was in the tiny guest room down the hall.

We couldn't get to sleep. The storm was so noisy. And we were both excited about the puppet skit and about finally being able to win against Anna and Maria.

I couldn't wait to see their faces when the three of us walked onstage with our puppets, and Anna and Maria realized that, for the first time ever, they were total losers.

Ha.

Bird finally fell asleep. I could hear his slow, steady breaths in the bunk beneath me. I stared at the ceiling, watching the bursts of light from the lightning flashes through the window.

I yawned, but I still didn't feel sleepy. I tried counting backward from one hundred. Sometimes that helps put me to sleep.

I was at seventy-two when I heard the sounds.

Soft thuds. A *clump clump clump* sound.

Coming from above my head?

I held my breath and listened, totally alert now.

*Clump clump scrape thud.*

Footsteps. Yes. Definitely. Footsteps. Above me. In the attic.

*Impossible*, I thought. And then my next thought was: *THE PUPPETS*.

Yes. I pictured them. The three marionettes, freed from the cabinet, walking around up there. Walking on their own.

Lying flat on my back, I balled my hands into tight fists. My whole body tensed, every muscle tight, as I listened.

I tried to *wish* the sounds away. I tried to tell myself it was the storm. The thunder. The rain pounding the roof.

I tried to convince myself it was my imagination.

It had to be.

But no.

*Bump bump thud.*

They were walking around up there. The princess, the sultan, the knight. It *had* to be them. But how was that possible?

*Clump clump clump.*

Right above my head. In the attic above my head.

I wanted to hide under the blanket, but I knew I had to go up there.

I kicked off the bed cover and dropped heavily to the floor. "Bird — wake up! Wake up!" I grabbed his shoulders with both hands and started to shake him.

He's a very deep sleeper. He groaned but didn't open his eyes.

"Wake up! Bird — come on! Bird! You've got to wake up!"

Finally, he raised his head from the pillow, blinking. "Huh? What's up? Is it morning?"

I grabbed a flashlight and jammed it into his hand. "Follow me! Hurry! It's the puppets!" I cried.

He shook his head. "What about the puppets?"

"You'll see." I tugged him to his feet. "Hurry."

I darted out into the hall. Clicked on my flashlight and followed the circle of light to the guest room. "Jenny! Wake up!" I tapped on the door. "Wake up!"

The door swung open. She was still in her jeans and sweater. She hadn't changed for bed. "I'm awake, Ben. What do you want?" she demanded.

"It's the puppets!" I cried. "I heard them. Walking around upstairs."

She grabbed my shoulder. "Take a breath. You're totally losing it."

"No. I'm not," I insisted. "You'll see. You'll see." I pulled away from her and trotted barefoot toward the door to the attic stairs.

Bird and Jenny followed close behind. "I knew we shouldn't have messed with puppets," she said. "I knew you would freak, Ben."

"I'm not!" I cried. "I'm telling you the truth. They're up there. You'll see."

45

I swung open the door and swept the beam of light up the stairs. The steps felt cold under my bare feet as I grabbed the shaky banister and pulled myself up.

"You'll see. You'll see."

My heart was pounding so hard my chest hurt as I reached the landing. I stepped into the attic, sweeping my light all around.

Bird and Jenny came right behind me. Our flashlights cut through the clutter of cartons and covered furniture.

"Oh, wow!" I cried. "Look!"

# 11

A creature. Moving fast. I saw the dark glow of its eyes. Its paws thudded over the attic floor.

Too stunned to move, I froze. And watched it leap onto the top of a carton, paws scraping and skidding. Then it dove back to the floor and came racing toward us.

"Whoa." I felt it brush my leg. Felt a thump on my bare foot. And then it spun around and hurtled back from where it had come.

"A squirrel!" Bird cried. He aimed his light beam down at the creature. The squirrel's eyes lit up like car headlights. Frantic, it bounced against one wall, tumbled into a carton, thumped its way to the cabinet holding the marionettes.

"How did a squirrel get up here?" Bird asked. "Must be a hole in the attic ceiling."

"Does your dad have a net or something?" Jenny asked. "How are we ever going to get it out of here?"

Bird scratched his head. "Open the window, maybe."

The squirrel darted back and forth in a panic. Its tail rose stiffly behind it. Its dark eyes glowed, wide with fright.

Bird raised the window at the far end of the attic. "Squirrel! Here, squirrel!" he called.

The terrified animal darted back and forth over the cartons. Jenny and I tried to chase it toward the open window. But we were only frightening it more.

Finally, it gave a wild leap — and vanished out into the night. Breathing hard, Bird instantly slammed the window shut. "Victory!" he choked out.

Jenny slapped my back. "Way to go, Ben. You heard a squirrel running around up here, and you went nuts. You didn't hear puppets walking around. You heard a squirrel."

I stared hard at the cabinet at the other end of the narrow room. Then I turned to my sister. "Are you *sure*?"

# 12

Mrs. O'Neal held auditions for the variety show after school in the auditorium. Everyone in the sixth grade had to try out. But only ten acts would be picked for the show. And, of course, only one act would win the five-hundred-dollar prize.

Was I *psyched*? Well, yes, I did want to win the money. But it was a lot more important to keep Anna and Maria from winning it.

Jenny, Bird, and I hid our puppets behind a curtain backstage. Then we hurried into the auditorium to take seats. We didn't want anyone to know we were doing a puppet skit. Mainly, it had to be a surprise for the two girls.

Kids were spread out over the first four or five rows of seats. Mrs. O'Neal was behind a podium at the side of the stage, pawing through some note cards.

I saw Anna's sneaker shoot out into the aisle, but I couldn't stop myself in time. And I tripped and fell face-forward onto the hard floor. I bounced once and felt the air whoosh out of my lungs.

"Oh, did I do that?" Anna asked with false innocence. "I'm so sorry, Ben. How clumsy of me."

Gasping for breath, I struggled to my feet. Down the row of seats, kids were laughing at me. I felt a burst of anger in my chest. I raised a fist. Was I really going to punch Anna?

*Wait for it. Wait for it, Ben,* I told myself. *You'll get your revenge up on stage.*

I must have been more tense than I knew. I've never punched anyone in my life. I took a deep breath and got myself in control.

"Wow, Anna, are those sneakers size twelve?" I said. "I always wondered why your nickname is Bigfoot."

"Your nickname is Shut Up," she said. She and Maria bumped knuckles.

"Good one," Maria told her friend.

"Ben, please take a seat," Mrs. O'Neal called from the stage. "We're about to begin the auditions."

Anna stuck her sneaker out again, but this time I dodged around it. I found Jenny and Bird at the far end of the third row and dropped down beside them.

Mrs. O'Neal called Shawn Klostner and Gabe Dudley to the stage. These two guys are the only sixth graders who wear their jeans real low, wear muscle shirts, and baseball caps on backward. Shawn and Gabe are always rapping in the lunch room and in the halls and before class and out in the parking lot. So guess what their act was? They rapped.

They called it "Middle School, Yo." It was pretty funny. Shawn was beatboxing while Gabe rapped the verse. And they slouched across the stage like rappers.

When they finished, the kids in the auditorium clapped and cheered. Mrs. O'Neal thanked them, but she had a sour look on her face, like she had eaten a lemon. I don't think it was her kind of music.

Anna and Maria were next. They came onstage with a boy and a girl marionette. The boy was dressed in a dark tuxedo. The girl had a red ballroom gown and red high-heeled shoes. The costumes weren't bad.

"We are going to demonstrate for you all the ancient art of puppetry," Maria announced. "Anna and I took lessons from a master puppeteer. And I hope you enjoy the sophisticated movements of our marionettes."

"Just get on with it," I muttered. In the seat beside me, Jenny laughed.

Mrs. O'Neal leaned on the podium and watched the two girls with a big smile on her face. Dance music started, and Mrs. O'Neal tapped her fingers in rhythm to the music.

Their puppets really did look like rag dolls or sock puppets on strings. Their heads were round, and the faces were painted on. Their hair was made of strips of orange and yellow felt. And the marionettes had half as many strings as ours.

I hate to say it, but Anna and Maria did a good job. The two puppets really did appear to be dancing together. They swayed together and spun and bowed and twirled. In perfect time to the dance music.

When the music stopped and the two puppets took deep bows, the auditorium rang with cheers and applause. At the podium, Mrs. O'Neal clapped, too. "That was wonderful, girls. Very creative and well-performed."

"Thank you," Anna said. "Maria and I would like to dedicate our performance to Suri Yukoshi, who taught us the fine art of puppeteering."

I groaned. Could they be any more obnoxious? The answer was yes.

"And if we win the five-hundred-dollar prize money," Anna said, "we are donating it to Suri Yukoshi's Doll Hospital so that children can have their puppets and dolls repaired for free."

"That's very generous of you," Mrs. O'Neal said. She glanced down at her notecards. "Next will be April Lewis, who will accompany herself on the keyboard and sing a song from the movie *Frozen*."

April wheeled her keyboard onto the stage. She had trouble plugging it into the amp, and Mrs. O'Neal hurried over to help her.

I turned to Jenny and Bird. "What made us think we could compete with Anna and Maria?" I said, shaking my head. "Did you see how good they were?"

Bird wiped his sweaty palms on the legs of his jeans. "We'll be better."

"What makes you say that?" I demanded. "They were perfect."

"We'll be *more* perfect," Bird said.

Onstage, April started to sing. She's very good, the best singer in the sixth grade. But I couldn't listen. I was thinking about our puppet skit, thinking about how crazy we were.

My stomach felt as if I'd swallowed a huge rock. The back of my neck was prickly and wet. My hands were ice cold.

Mrs. O'Neal called us up next.

I trudged after Jenny and Bird to the stage. "We're doomed," I muttered. "Doomed."

"Come on, Ben," Jenny said. "Let's do our best."

"What have we got to lose?" Bird said.

I followed them to the back of the stage, where we had hidden our puppets. Bird pulled open the curtain. And all three of us gasped.

The puppets were gone.

# 13

I blinked several times, thinking that would make them reappear. "Whoa." I grabbed Bird's shoulder. "This is where we hid them — right?"

He nodded. His mouth hung open, and I saw drops of sweat on his forehead.

Jenny pulled the curtain open more and stepped behind it. "They — they're not here," she stammered.

I heard Mrs. O'Neal's voice from the podium at the front of the stage. "Ben? Jenny? You guys? Is there a problem?"

I stuck my head out from behind the curtain. "We . . . uh . . . can't find our puppets," I said.

For some reason, that made the kids in the auditorium erupt with laughter.

"We set them down right back here," Jenny told Mrs. O'Neal. "But they're not here now."

"Well, they didn't walk away on their own," Mrs. O'Neal said.

Her words made the breath catch in my throat.

*Walk away on their own.*

I was trying to get over my problem with puppets. But . . . puppets coming alive and walking on their own was one of my worst nightmares. The night I heard footsteps up in Bird's attic suddenly flashed back into my mind. Was it a squirrel I heard? Or had the puppets come to life?

Was I living my worst nightmare now?

"Are these what you're looking for?" Mrs. O'Neal asked. She had walked to the side of the stage and had the knight puppet draped over one arm.

"Yes," I said. "How did they get over there?"

I saw the other two puppets in a sitting position against the stage wall. The three of us trotted across the stage and picked up our puppets. Then we walked them to the center of the stage.

I tried to ignore my shaking legs and the chills that made me want to drop the puppet and run away. They hadn't walked on their own. *Someone moved them,* I told myself. *It's no big deal. Someone saw them behind the curtain and moved them to the side of the stage.*

I had the sultan puppet. I straightened his turban. Then I steadied the control sticks between my hands. Jenny and Bird were watching me, waiting for me to start the skit.

"*Hello, slaves,*" I made the sultan say in a raspy, shrill voice, raising his hands above his head. "*I am the king. See how I walk like a king?*"

I made the puppet strut in front of the princess and the knight.

Bird made the knight raise his sword. "I am a knight because I have a sword!" he boomed. "If you had a sword like mine —"

Suddenly, Bird stopped and stared into the audience.

I turned and saw what he was staring at. Anna and Maria had jumped to their feet and were waving wildly to Mrs. O'Neal.

"Sit down, girls." Mrs. O'Neal motioned with both hands. "Don't interrupt their skit."

"But this isn't right!" Maria cried. "They can't do puppets."

"They *knew* we were doing puppets," Anna said. "And they are just copying us."

"Sit down right now," the teacher snapped. "I really think there's room in our show for *two* puppet acts."

"But it's not *fair*!" Maria whined. "We took lessons and everything."

"Let them finish!" a boy shouted from the back of the auditorium. And then other kids instantly took up the chant: "Let them finish! Let them finish!"

Anna and Maria's faces were an angry red. They glared at us, scowling. Then they sank slowly into their seats.

I grinned at Bird and Jenny. "That was

awesome," I whispered. "Did you see the looks on their faces? We already won!"

When the kids in the audience finally stopped chanting, we did our skit. We were getting big laughs and a few cheers. I kept glancing at Anna and Maria. They sat stiffly with their arms crossed in front of them. Their faces were still bright red.

At the end of the skit, we made our puppets take deep bows. Then we carried them offstage.

Mrs. O'Neal grinned at us, with two thumbs raised. "That was excellent," she said. "Very enjoyable." She turned to Anna and Maria. "We definitely have room for two puppet acts. Especially since the puppets are so different."

"But we were *first*!" Anna declared.

Mrs. O'Neal ignored her and studied her little name cards. Then she raised her eyes to us. "Why don't you all take your marionettes to the art room, where they will be safe. Then come back and watch the rest of the auditions."

Anna and Maria grumbled to one another as they edged down the aisle and went to collect their puppets at the side of the stage. We followed them down to the art room at the end of the hall, but they pretended we weren't there.

"I liked your puppet dance," Jenny said to them. Jenny always has to be nice.

"Of course you did. It's awesome," Anna replied. Maria just sneered.

We hurried back to see the other auditions. Vanessa Arthur was onstage, doing a baton-twirling act. I took a seat at the end of an aisle and tried to concentrate.

But my mind was spinning with images and thoughts. I kept thinking about our puppets and how easy they were to operate. I kept going over the skit we had just performed, remembering what the kids in the audience had laughed at the hardest.

Once again, I had the strange feeling that I had seen these puppets before. My sister said she had the same feeling. But neither of us could remember where or when we'd seen them.

We both had the same weird problem with puppets. So we never went to puppet shows. And we never watched puppets on TV. Even the Muppets made me feel shaky and a little afraid.

I found myself thinking about Bird's dad. *We should have told Coach Sparrow that we were taking his puppets to school,* I told myself. Why was Bird so afraid we would get into trouble? He definitely refused to tell his dad what we were doing. Bird said we could tell him *after* we won the five-hundred-dollar prize.

After Vanessa, four guys came onstage break-dancing. Kids were clapping with the beats and cheering them on.

I glanced down the aisle and saw Anna and Maria still glaring angrily at me.

*Give it a rest,* I thought. Were they going to keep those sour expressions on their faces for the rest of their lives?

"That's our last audition," Mrs. O'Neal announced as the dancers trotted off to a deafening ovation. They raised their fists above their heads in triumph. One of the guys did a crazy somersault and almost fell off the stage.

"So many great acts," Mrs. O'Neal said, tapping her stack of cards against the podium. "Thank you all for staying after school. I'll announce the ten acts for the variety show later this week."

Everyone jumped up and started to make their way up the aisles to the auditorium doors at the back. I met up with Bird and Jenny in the hall and we headed to the art room to collect the marionettes.

"Nice job, Ben." Someone tapped me on the shoulder. I turned to see Vanessa Arthur smiling at me. *Wow,* I thought. *That's the first time she ever talked to me!*

"You did a great job with the baton," I said.

Her smile grew wider. "Yeah. I only dropped it once."

Jenny, Bird, and I arrived at the art room at the same time as Anna and Maria. They took a few steps into the room — then stopped.

I saw Anna's eyes go wide and her mouth drop open. Maria gasped.

Then they both let out screams of horror.

"I don't *believe* it!" Anna shrieked. "How *could* you?!"

"No way! No *way*! How could you do this?" Maria cried, her hands pressed to her cheeks.

We pushed past them to see what they were staring at. I saw their puppets, the boy and the girl, facedown on the floor. It took me a few seconds to realize that their strings had been cut.

"No way! No way!" Maria repeated.

Anna started to cry, big tears rolling down her cheeks.

I couldn't believe it, either. Jenny and Bird stepped up to the puppets and bent down to examine them. Yes, the strings had all been cut.

"How could you do this?" Anna demanded through her tears. "You were so jealous of us? You had to ruin our puppets?"

"I — I —" I stammered. "We didn't do it!" I finally managed to choke out.

And then my eyes caught the sultan puppet. It was slouched on the chair where I'd left it. Its head was tilted back, a wide smile on its face. And grasped in its hand . . .

In its hand I saw a large pair of scissors.

# 14

Ms. Feeney is the new principal at our school. Our old principal was a hundred and twelve. But Ms. Feeney is young, and has long wavy blond hair and wears bright red lipstick, and she dresses in jeans and T-shirts, which makes everyone think she is cool and awesome and terrific.

Even though she was so awesome and terrific, I didn't want to be sitting in her office beside Bird and Jenny. We sat on folding chairs across from her desk, and she kept giving us the eye, studying us one by one as if she could see into our brains.

The office was small and kind of cramped, and hot. I kept wiping sweat off my forehead. I kept my eyes on the desk photo of her golden Lab. I didn't want to catch her hard stare. Beside me, Bird kept wiping his palms on the legs of his jeans and tapping his fingers rapidly.

Jenny had her hands clasped tightly in her lap. She kept biting her lower lip. She only does that when she's really stressed out.

Anna and Maria were huddled on the couch in the outer office. Through the open door, I could see that Anna was still crying. Maria had an arm around her shoulders, trying to comfort her.

It was silent for a long while as Ms. Feeney eyed us one by one. Then she chewed on the end of a pencil for a while. Finally, she brushed back her blond hair and spoke: "So does anyone want to tell me what happened in the art room a few minutes ago?" She speaks softly, almost in a whisper.

Anna sobbed in the outer office.

"We didn't do it. I swear," I said, raising my right hand.

Ms. Feeney squinted at me. "You didn't sneak back to the art room and vandalize their puppets?"

"Ms. Feeney, we never left the auditorium," Jenny said. "We watched all the auditions."

"It's true," Bird chimed in. "Why would we cut the strings on their puppets? Their puppets are lame."

"That's beside the point," the principal said, frowning. "You say you didn't do it. But someone did. Someone went into the art room, cut the strings on the two puppets, and placed the scissors in the other puppet's hand."

"It wasn't us —" I insisted.

"Someone must have thought that was a funny joke," the principal said. "Putting the scissors in the puppet's hand. Making it look like the puppet did it."

"Maybe he did," I said. The words fell out of my mouth. I didn't think about them first.

I immediately regretted it. I could feel my face turning red.

Ms. Feeney squinted at me. "Excuse me?"

"I didn't mean to say that," I replied.

Ms. Feeney leaned across the desk. Her eyes locked on mine. "Do you want me to believe that your puppet walked across the room and cut the strings on the girls' marionettes? Do you seriously think you are living in some kind of science-fiction movie where puppets come alive?"

"Well . . . no," I stammered. I could feel my face growing hot and knew I was blushing.

"Let me explain," Jenny chimed in. "Ben has always had a weird thing about puppets. Me too. He doesn't really believe the puppets are alive."

Ms. Feeney sighed and tapped the pencil against the chair arm. "Someone did this terrible prank, and it wasn't a puppet."

"We know," Bird said. "But I promise it wasn't us."

Ms. Feeney nodded. She brushed her blond hair back off her shoulders. "I believe you. I don't think you did it. But I don't know who else it could have been."

"We never left the auditorium," I said. "We never —"

She raised a hand to silence me. "No more incidents like this," she said. "You understand me, right? If something else happens, you'll automatically be out of Mrs. O'Neal's show. And I'll have to call your parents in for a serious talk."

The three of us nodded.

"No problem," Bird muttered.

Ms. Feeney waved us out of her office. She called to Anna and Maria. "Okay, girls, you can come in now."

"Did you suspend them from school?" Anna asked as she brushed past us. "That's what I would do."

I didn't hear the principal's reply. Jenny, Bird, and I hurried away from her office. We stopped near the front doors to the school. "That was a close one," I said.

Jenny and Bird nodded. Jenny frowned at me. "It got especially tense when you started talking about how the puppets are alive. What were you trying to prove? That you're totally insane?"

I shrugged. "I just lost it for a moment."

Bird pounded his fist against the wall. "Well . . . who did it? We know we didn't. Our puppet skit was a major hit. Everyone loved it.

Why would we want to wreck the girls' lame puppets? No way."

"Maybe it was someone else who auditioned," I said, thinking hard. "You know. Someone who's afraid of not getting in the show. So they wanted to make sure Anna and Maria couldn't be in it."

"That's crazy," Jenny said. "Do you think someone really wants the five hundred dollars that badly?"

I shrugged again. "I'm totally confused. I mean, nothing makes sense to me."

"Let's get the puppets and get out of here," Bird said.

We turned the corner and made our way down the empty, silent hall to the art room at the end. I followed Bird and Jenny into the room. I saw our marionettes sprawled at the table where we left them.

Then I turned and saw what Jenny and Bird were staring at.

"Oh, no! Oh, wow!" I gasped. "This can't be happening! Who is *doing* this?"

# 15

PUPPETS RULE!

My mouth dropped open as I stared at the words scrawled across the wall in huge, ragged black letters. "Nooooo," I moaned.

"Who would do this?" Jenny asked in a tiny voice, her hands pressed to the sides of her face. "Who?" She gazed from Bird to me, as if we had the answer.

Bird shrugged. "We're in major trouble." He was suddenly pale and he kept blinking rapidly, eyes on the smeared black words.

"Is it black paint?" My question came out in a whisper.

"I think it's marker," Jenny said.

Then I turned — and gaped at the large black marker in the princess puppet's hand. "NO WAY!" I choked out.

All three of us staggered over to the puppet, who was sitting very straight in a chair at one of the art tables. Two black markers were open in front of the puppet on the table. And one appeared to be gripped in her right hand.

I heard footsteps out in the hall. The sound made all my muscles tighten.

Ms. Feeney?

"Hurry," Jenny said, running to the sink at the far wall. "Get sponges. Maybe we can scrub the words off before anyone sees them."

Bird trotted after her to the sink. But I didn't move. I *couldn't* move.

I couldn't take my eyes off the puppet. I kept staring at the sly smile on her wooden face. At her shiny green eyes that appeared to be laughing at me. My gaze stopped on the marker attached to her right hand.

"I told you," I muttered.

Bird and Jenny dragged stools to the wall and started wiping wet sponges over the scrawled words. "It . . . isn't coming off," Jenny said.

"I told you," I repeated. "I know you think I'm crazy — but these puppets are alive."

"Shut up, Ben," Jenny said.

"No one else could have done this," I insisted. "There are no kids still in school. Just a few teachers and the principal. The puppet did it. It can't be anyone else."

"Shut up and come help us," Jenny said, scrubbing with both hands. Gray water from the sponges ran down the green tile wall. But the words hadn't faded at all.

Bird turned to me. "Ben, you've got to stop thinking like that. It's too crazy. Puppets don't come alive. And no one is going to believe that a puppet grabbed a marker and wrote these words. No one."

"Okay, okay," I muttered.

The princess puppet stared up at me with that sly grin on her face.

I swallowed hard. *You aren't alive*, I thought. *You CAN'T be alive.*

I reached down to her hand to take the black marker away —

— and she wouldn't let go of it!

# 16

"No way!" I shrieked. "No way!"

Jenny and Bird jumped off their stools and came running over to me. "What's wrong?" Jenny demanded.

"The m-marker —" I stammered, pointing with a trembling finger.

Jenny wrapped her hand around the marker and lifted it easily from the puppet's hand. "Yes? What about the marker?" She raised it to my face.

"The princess. She . . . wouldn't let go of it," I said. "I tried to take it and —"

"It was stuck, that's all," Jenny said.

"Don't totally freak, Ben," Bird said. "We've got enough trouble without you losing it."

And as he said that, I heard a sound at the art room door. A cough.

I spun around and saw Ms. Feeney enter the room. "Are you kids still here?" she asked. Her eyes moved to the black marker in Jenny's hand.

And then she raised her gaze to the two words scrawled in black on the art room wall.

Her mouth formed a small O. She blinked a few times. Then she squinted again at the marker in Jenny's hand.

"I'll see you in my office," Ms. Feeney said finally. "And please don't tell me the puppets did it."

# PART TWO

# ONE WEEK LATER

# 17

Jenny, Bird, and I were suspended from school for a week. And, of course, we were kicked out of the variety show.

We called our long week at home *Doom Week*. Only, it was worse than doom.

Can you imagine how thrilled our parents were to be called to school to meet with Mrs. O'Neal and Ms. Feeney? And how do you think they liked it when the teacher and the principal described the three of us as "destructive problem children"?

I don't really know what happened at Bird's house. Coach Sparrow must have been shocked that the puppets were at school and not in the hidden cabinet. He probably got on Bird's case about taking them without telling him. But Jenny and I had no idea what happened at their house across the street.

We didn't talk to Bird for the whole week, because we weren't allowed to talk to anyone from school. Our phones were taken away. We weren't allowed to text or email anyone on our laptops.

Talk about grounded.

We were forbidden to do anything that might be a little fun. Every electronic thing Jenny and I owned was unplugged.

And maybe the worst part of Doom Week was the heart-to-heart talks we were forced to have with our parents every night after dinner. Long discussions about how we felt about school and why we did those horrible things in the art room, and how it would never happen again.

Of course, Jenny and I told them over and over that we were totally innocent. That we didn't cut the puppets' strings and we didn't paint *Puppets Rule* on the wall. We shouted. We pleaded. We practically jumped up and down on the furniture.

Did they believe us?

Three guesses.

The teacher and the principal said Jenny and Bird and I did those crimes, and that was good enough for our parents.

And so Doom Week slowly . . . slooooooowly dragged on.

And now, a week later, we eagerly burst out of our home-prison and jogged all the way to school, backpacks bouncing on our backs. I wondered if kids would make fun of us, or look at us funny, or keep away from us, like we were criminals or something. But kids didn't treat Bird, Jenny, and me any differently at all. In fact, most of them didn't seem to realize we had been gone!

The morning was going great. We were so glad to be back. Nothing much happened ... until lunch period. That's when we bumped into Anna and Maria walking into the lunch room.

They stepped in front of us to keep us from joining the cafeteria line. They both had these wide grins on their faces.

"I hear you have some evil puppets on your hands," Anna said, sticking her grinning face close to mine.

"Just leave us alone," I muttered. I tried to squirm past them, but they stepped quickly to block my path.

"Go away," Bird said. "Give us a break."

"How did you like being suspended from school for a week?" Maria demanded. "It never happened to *me*. I just wonder what it was like."

"Shut up," I said. "We just want to get some lunch."

"That's rude," Maria said. "Don't you want to chat with us?"

"No."

"I hear your puppets are really good with scissors and black marker," Anna said. "That's totally amazing!"

I stared hard at them. Stared, my mind churning. And suddenly I realized what had happened. Suddenly, everything became clear.

"YOU did it!" I screamed. "You two did it — *didn't* you?!"

Their grins grew wider.

Bird's mouth dropped open. "Is Ben right?" he demanded. "You cut your own puppets' strings — just to get us kicked out of the show?"

They exchanged glances. Then they both burst out laughing.

"You *did*!" I cried. "Admit it. Admit it! You cut the puppets' strings just to get us in trouble. You wrecked your own puppets."

Anna's grin stayed frozen on her face. "It only takes ten minutes to put new strings on puppets, dumb head."

I gasped. I couldn't breathe.

"And the words on the wall?" Jenny said.

Anna and Maria nodded. "Your puppets were very naughty," Maria said.

"You — you — you got us suspended from school," Bird stammered, his face red with anger. "You got us grounded for a week. You got us in so much trouble."

"Have a great lunch," Anna said. They turned and started to walk away. They both couldn't stop laughing.

After a few steps, Anna turned around. "If you tell on us, no one will believe you," she said.

"You know I'm right." She spun away and hurried to catch up with her friend.

I stood watching them walk away. I was gritting my teeth so hard, my jaw ached. Every muscle in my body was tensed and tight. I felt the anger in my chest and imagined steam pouring from my ears.

Jenny and Bird appeared frozen in shock. I turned to them and in a trembling whisper, I choked out: "This means WAR."

# 18

After dinner Friday night, Jenny and I ran across the street to Bird's house. Coach Sparrow was away at his soccer team practice. The three of us hurried up to the attic to pull the marionettes from the cabinet.

I realized my heart was racing and my hands felt cold and sweaty. I just couldn't get over my lingering fear of puppets. These puppets had already landed us in major trouble. I knew it wasn't their fault. I knew thinking that they were actually alive wasn't just crazy — it was stupid.

But still . . .

The strings on all three puppets had become tangled when we returned them to the cabinet. We spread them out on their backs on the attic floor and worked at untangling them.

"Tell me again," Jenny said to me. "Why exactly are we doing this? Why are we rehearsing our skit again?"

"Yeah. Explain," Bird repeated. "You know what my dad said. He said —"

"I know what your dad said," I interrupted. "He told us a hundred times not to use these puppets."

Bird's eyes locked on mine. "And you *do* remember that Mrs. O'Neal kicked us out of the variety show?"

"I know, I know," I replied. One of the strings to the sultan's head had a tight knot in it. Squinting in the dim attic light, I struggled to loosen it.

"So why are we up here rehearsing our puppet skit?" Bird demanded.

"We're going to photo-bomb the variety show," I said.

Jenny laughed. "You mean *puppet*-bomb the show?"

I nodded. I couldn't keep a grin from my face. I knew my idea was brilliant and awesome, if I didn't say so myself.

"We're going to sneak to the side of the stage during the variety show," I explained. "Then we're going to run onstage and do our skit."

Bird raised a hand. "But — but —"

"Once we're out there, how can Mrs. O'Neal stop us?" I said, waving him down. "Is she going to drag us off one by one? Of course not. Once we start, there's *no way* she can stop us."

"But we can't win the prize money," Jenny said. "We can't —"

"That doesn't matter," I told her. "This is all about *revenge*. Our puppets are so awesome, and our skit is totally funny. Let's say Anna and Maria win the grand prize. *Everyone* will know that we were better. Even if they win, WE win!"

Jenny and Bird thought about it for a moment. Then Bird cracked a smile, and his little bird eyes lit up. "Excellent plan, dude."

Jenny frowned. "We could get into trouble again."

"But it would be worth it," I said. "Anna and Maria spoiled everything for us. Now it's our turn to spoil it for them."

Jenny shrugged. "Okay. Let's do it."

It took a while to get the strings untangled and the knots out. Then we made the knight, the princess, and the sultan stand, and we started to rehearse. It was easy to get back to the skit, especially since we had rehearsed for so long for our audition.

We had some funny new ideas. In one, the knight deliberately gets his strings tangled up with the princess. The sultan tries to separate them, and he gets tangled up, too.

It was a tricky thing to do, because we didn't really want the strings to become tangled. But when we finally got it right, it looked very funny. And we made up a lot of great dialogue for the three mixed-up puppets.

The three of us were feeling pretty good. And as we worked the skit out, our revenge plan seemed better and better. We rehearsed for nearly two hours. Then Jenny and Bird went downstairs to get some snacks and drinks.

And that's when something weird happened.

# 19

I was dancing the sultan back and forth down the narrow attic. I made him raise both hands above his head, and then I had him kick his legs high in the air, one at a time, kick . . . kick . . . kick . . . in a wild rhythmic dance.

I'm not sure if I tripped over the puppet or if I just lost my balance. I had the strangest feeling that the puppet tripped *me*. But, of course, that was ridiculous.

Anyway, the next thing I knew, I was down on the floor. I hit hard on my left side and pain shot up from my elbow. The sultan puppet collapsed on top of me. The head and the turban bounced against my side, and its arms fell limply around me, as if wrapping me in a loose hug.

"Ohhhhh." I uttered a low moan and waited for the pain in my arm to fade.

Then I started to pull myself up. But the puppet was in an awkward position. I mean, it felt as if it was pushing me down. Yes. Crazy. I know. But the two hands pressed against my side.

And then the sultan's head moved. It bobbed once. Twice. And raised itself toward my face.

I tried to shake my head clear. I knew I was just feeling a little weird because of my fall. I knew the puppet wasn't climbing over me, both little hands grabbling at my sweatshirt.

"Whoa! Wait!"

I cried out as I felt the puppet's long nose poke at my ear. I struggled to push the sultan off me. But the wooden nose bobbed and bumped my ear.

And then I felt it poke inside. Inside my ear. And I felt a strange tingle. Almost like an electric shock. I heard a buzzing sound and felt a strong vibration.

"Nooooo!" I uttered a cry, grabbed the puppet by its shoulders — and heaved it off me. The nose slid out of my ear with a loud *crackle*.

"Ben — what's up?"

For one second, I thought the sultan said that. But then I saw Bird at the top of the attic stairs, carrying cans of Coke, and staring across the room at me on the floor with the puppet gripped in both hands.

"I . . . uh . . . tripped," I said. I climbed up quickly. I held the puppet by the waist. Its head and hands hung limply down. "I tripped over the puppet and fell." I rubbed my arm. "Landed on my funny bone."

"Ouch," Jenny said, crossing the room with a large bag of tortilla chips and a bowl of salsa. "Are you okay?"

I nodded. "I guess."

I could still feel the electric tingling in my ear. My whole body seemed to buzz. I shook myself, trying to force the sound away.

I took the bag of tortilla chips from my sister, tore it open, and grabbed a handful. I suddenly felt unbelievably hungry, as if I hadn't eaten in days. We sat down with our backs against the attic wall and had our snack time.

A few minutes later, we put aside the chips and the soda cans and picked up our marionettes. We were just starting to rehearse again when Bird's dad burst into the attic.

He was still in his soccer sweatshirt. The front was stained with sweat. His coach's whistle dangled from a cord around his neck.

When he saw us, his eyes bulged and his mouth opened in an O of shock.

"Those puppets? You took them out again?" he cried, pointing at the marionettes with a trembling finger. "I *told* you to put them in the cabinet and leave them there. I *pleaded* with you not to take them out."

He narrowed his eyes at us. "Don't you realize we're now in danger? All of us — we're in terrible danger!"

Coach Sparrow lumbered toward us, shaking his head. He kept his eyes on the three puppets in our hands.

"I told you last week," he said, "I hid them away years ago. I knew I should have destroyed them."

"But — why, Dad?" Bird demanded. "What's wrong with them? You keep telling us not to use them. But you won't tell us why."

Coach Sparrow started to talk, but his voice faded from my ears. I suddenly had a flash of memory. Something had been troubling me since we found the puppets. Something had been pushing at the back of my mind. And now I saw it so clearly.

"Jenny," I said. "These are the puppets from our birthday party!"

"Excuse me?" She squinted at me. "Birthday party?"

"Yes," I said, unable to hide my excitement.

"Our party when we were five. I just remembered them."

"Oh, wow," Jenny murmured. "Wow. Wow. You're right." She raised her eyes to Bird's dad. "These puppets terrified everyone at our party. We were all crying."

"That's right," I said. "I remember it all now. There was a puppeteer at the party. An old man. He had a long white beard."

"Yes. I remember him, too," Jenny said. "When the puppets made everyone cry, he went berserk. He grabbed up his puppets and ran out of the house."

"I remember it, too," Coach Sparrow said softly.

The three of us turned to him. "Why do *you* remember it?" I asked.

"Because I was the old puppeteer," he replied.

He walked to the cabinet, reached inside, and pulled out the fake white beard. He held it up to his face. "See? It was *me* at your birthday party."

Jenny and I stared hard at him. The memories of that frightening day came rushing back. And now we held the three puppets that had terrified us so badly.

Bird was the first to speak. "Dad? You were a puppeteer?"

Coach Sparrow sighed. "Well, I wanted to be an entertainer back then. I was already teaching. But I thought I could pick up extra money by doing shows at kids' birthday parties. But it didn't work out . . ." His voice trailed off.

"Where'd you get these puppets?" Bird asked him. "Did you make them?"

"Make them? No. I bought them from a puppet-maker on the other side of town. I brought them home and practiced with them, trying to come up with a funny act for kids. Ben and Jenny's birthday party was the first puppet show I ever gave."

He sighed again. "The first and the last."

"I don't understand," I said. "I remember the puppets bit us and hurt us. Was that supposed to be funny?"

Bird's dad shook his head. "Of course not. I . . . I can't really explain, Ben. I only know that I lost control of them. They didn't do what I tried to make them do."

Coach Sparrow shook his head, remembering. "It scared me to death. It was like they were . . . ALIVE."

A hush fell over the attic. Jenny, Bird, and I were still holding our puppets by their control sticks. I set mine down on the floor and took a step back from it.

"The birthday party was a disaster." Coach Sparrow continued his story. "I grabbed the puppets up into my arms as fast as I could. I had to stop them before they hurt more kids. I grabbed them and ran home. And I locked the puppets away up here and hid the cabinet behind a stack of cartons. I knew I'd never use them again."

He mopped his forehead with the sleeve of his soccer jersey. He shuddered. I guess he was remembering how frightened he had been.

"Why didn't you just throw them in the trash?" Bird demanded.

"I thought about it," his dad replied. "But what if someone else found them? What if someone gave them to children and then the children were hurt by them? I decided it was safer to lock them up and keep them hidden."

I shuddered. Once again, I remembered feeling the sultan puppet's wooden nose poking into my ear. *We should have left these puppets locked up.*

Coach Sparrow had a faraway look in his eyes. "I wanted to give them back to the puppet-maker," he said. "I was *desperate* to give them back to him. And to ask him why the puppets went out of control."

He shook his head again. "But I lost the man's address. I searched the neighborhood across town, but I couldn't find his building. I tried everything. But I couldn't find him."

Bird made the knight puppet bounce up and down on the floor. Then he made the puppet take a bow.

"Stop. We have to hide the puppets away," Coach Sparrow insisted. "Hand them to me. We have to lock them up again — before it's too late." He bent down and lifted the sultan puppet off the floor and tossed it over his shoulder.

"But we *need* them," Bird cried. "We need them for school. You can't lock them away. Just let us do our show with them. Then we'll bring them right home and lock them up again for good. I promise."

"Not happening," Coach Sparrow said. He took the princess controls from Jenny. "Not happening. Maybe the puppets haven't done anything evil so far. But they *will*! Trust me. They *will*!"

The three of us argued with him some more. But we could see he wouldn't change his mind.

We watched helplessly as he hung the puppets in the cabinet. Then he shut the cabinet doors tight and fastened the metal latch. "Stay away from them," he said, gazing from Bird to Jenny to me. "I'm serious. Don't let these puppets out again."

We watched him cross the attic. No one said a word until he lumbered down the stairs and was out of sight.

I dropped onto the floor with a sigh, then rested my back against the attic wall. "So much for *that* great plan," I muttered.

Bird ran a hand back through his hair. "We're ruined. We have no act. Anna and Maria win again."

I had my arms crossed in front of me. Suddenly, my hands shot up above my head. "Hey!" I let out a startled cry.

"Ben — what are you doing?" Jenny demanded.

My arms sank limply at my sides.

My heart started to race. "I . . . didn't mean to do that," I stammered.

My arms felt weird. Kind of light and weak. And my hands suddenly felt heavy, as if they'd put on weight.

"Whoa." Both hands rose up above my head again. And my legs kicked up and down.

Bird laughed. "Dude, you look like a puppet."

"Stop doing that, Ben." Jenny grabbed my left arm and tugged it down. But it shot right up again. "You're not funny," Jenny said. "Stop it. You're scaring me."

*It's scaring me, too,* I thought. *What is happening to me?*

# 21

Bright yellow sunlight through my bedroom window woke me up on Saturday morning. I blinked a few times, glanced at the clock on my bed table. Nine twenty.

My stomach rumbled. I don't usually sleep that late.

I tried to raise my head from the pillow. It felt heavier than usual. It took a hard pull to raise it a few inches.

I blinked some more. My eyelids slid up and down. I tried to stop them, but they kept on blinking.

*What's up with that?*

I started to kick my covers off. But my legs felt weak. My kick was too soft to move the blanket. I concentrated and tried again. My legs felt kind of rubbery, as if I had no bones.

Still blinking, I sat up. I guessed I'd slept in a bad position. You know the tingling feeling you get in your hand when you've slept on top of it? That's what my whole body felt like.

I finally stood up, but my knees kept bending. I stretched my hands above my head. Gave myself a good stretch. *Yes.* I was starting to feel more like myself.

I pulled on yesterday's jeans and a T-shirt from the pile of shirts on my closet floor. Then I made my way to the kitchen for breakfast.

Jenny sat at the table with her face nearly dunking into a big bowl of Corn Flakes. She looked up as I entered. "Mom and Dad went grocery shopping. They said they might be gone all morning." She had a ring of milk around her mouth and down her chin.

I took the cereal box off the counter and started toward my place at the table. But my legs bent and I nearly dropped the box. I struggled to walk straight. But I kept bobbing up and down the way a marionette walks.

Jenny squinted at me from behind her Corn Flakes bowl. "Why are you doing that? Are you trying to be funny?"

I didn't want to tell her I was having major problems. I didn't want to freak her out until I could figure out what was wrong with me.

"Yeah. I'm trying to be funny," I said.

She rolled her eyes. "Hilarious."

My arms felt stiff and weak. I had to grip the cereal box in both hands. My hands felt floppy, almost as if they had no bones.

A chill of fear ran down my back. *Something is very wrong.*

I forced a smile to my face. I didn't want to frighten Jenny. I wished Mom and Dad were home. Maybe I was getting the flu or something. Maybe I needed to see Dr. Ackerman.

I poured some Corn Flakes into a bowl. Then I reached for the milk carton. But both of my hands shot up over my head. They dangled up there like puppet hands.

Jenny squinted at me from across the table. "Why are you even weirder than usual this morning?" she asked.

"Dunno," I muttered. I was suddenly too frightened to give a sarcastic answer. "Dunno."

My mouth slid up and down stiffly. I tried to move my lips, but they felt stiff, too. My jaw wouldn't slide from side to side. It would only move up and down.

"Put your arms down," Jenny said. "You're not funny, Ben. You're just weird."

*I have to tell her what's happening to me*, I decided.

"Jenny, I'm not trying to be funny," I said. The words came out garbled because my mouth wouldn't move right. My teeth kept clicking after every word.

"I'm not trying to be funny," I repeated. "I . . . I don't feel right. I think I'm . . . turning into a puppet."

She set down her cereal spoon and studied me. Then she burst out laughing.

# 22

"Jenny, please —" I started.

She laughed till she had tears in her eyes. She wiped them with her napkin. "Ben, you were really starting to scare me. All that hands-waving-in-the-air stuff. You totally fooled me."

I wanted to grit my teeth, but my mouth would only open and close. "I'm . . . not . . . joking," I managed to choke out.

She shook her head. "Enough. Seriously." Then her eyes flashed. "Oh, wait. Maybe that's an *awesome* idea, Ben. We can't use those puppets. But maybe we could *be* puppets. We could pretend to be puppets. I'll bet we could be a riot. We could —"

"Jenny, I'm not pretending!" I cried. The words came out tinny and shrill. Suddenly, I had a puppet voice. I pressed my hands against my cheeks. They felt smooth and hard.

Like wood!

My skin was turning to wood!

I stretched my hands across the table. "Feel them!" I insisted. "Go ahead. Feel my hands."

She hesitated. Then she reached out both of her hands and squeezed mine. The smile quickly faded from her face. "They're . . . hard," she murmured.

"Feel my face," I said. "Go ahead. Rub my cheeks."

"You . . . you're starting to scare me."

"*I'm* the one who's scared!" I cried in my tinny puppet voice.

She rubbed the back of one hand against my face. "Oh, wow." Her eyes bulged with horror. "Oh no. Oh, I don't believe this."

She closed her hand in a fist and tapped it against my forehead. It made a clonking sound, like knocking on wood.

Jenny jumped to her feet. "We've got to get Mom and Dad. You're sick or something. Mom has her cell. We have to call her right away."

My hands waved in the air. "You'd better do it," I said. "I don't think I can hold a phone."

Jenny ran and got her phone and punched in Mom's number. After a few seconds, she clicked it off. "It went right to voicemail. I . . . I just remembered something. Mom was upset because she forgot to charge it last night. And Dad's phone is broken, remember?"

"You mean we can't reach them?" I cried, my lips clicking.

Jenny shook her head. "We'll have to wait —"

"NO!" I cried. "We can't wait." I struggled to think. My eyes slid from side to side. I realized I couldn't move them up and down. My wooden head started to feel heavy.

"Coach Sparrow," I said. I struggled to my feet. "He'll help me."

"Yes!" Jenny cried. "Good plan."

She had to help me put on my sneakers. Then she had to help me cross the street. My legs kept folding beneath me. My head bobbed, and my arms were totally out of my control.

Bird greeted us at the front door. He appeared very surprised to see us so early. "What's up?"

"We need to see your dad," Jenny said.

"He's not here," Bird said. "He had early soccer practice."

"NOOOOO!" A hoarse cry escaped my throat.

I lost it. I totally lost it. I couldn't hold in my fear — my *terror* — any longer.

"Ben, what's your problem?" Bird demanded.

I didn't answer. I shoved him out of my way and staggered into his house. I tripped and stumbled through the living room, making my way to the back hall.

The aroma of bacon floated in from the kitchen. I tripped over the coffee table, sending a pile of books tumbling to the floor.

"Where are you going? What are you doing?" Bird demanded. He and Jenny chased after me.

My puppet legs collapsed, and I fell to the floor. My wooden head bounced on the carpet.

"Ben has a problem," I heard Jenny tell Bird. "Something weird is happening to him. He needs a doctor."

"No —" I choked out.

I knew what I needed. I needed to get upstairs to those puppets. It all came clear to me. It didn't take a genius to realize why this was happening to me.

That sultan puppet. He'd pushed his nose into my ear. I had felt the strong electric shock. The shock that ran down my whole body.

*That puppet did this to me.* Coach Sparrow was right. The three puppets *were* alive. They were alive — and they wanted to turn us into puppets, too.

Had they been real kids at one time?

I didn't care. I had only one thing in mind. Grab the sultan puppet and force it to turn me back into myself.

I scrambled up the attic stairs. I don't know how I made it all the way up. I kept stumbling and landing on my stomach. But I *had* to get up there. My life depended on it.

Morning sunlight washed through the dust-smeared attic window. The floorboards creaked as the three of us hurried to the cabinet at the far wall.

"My dad said not to open the cabinet," Bird said, reaching for my shoulder.

I ducked out of his grasp. My puppet hands were already on the latch. I swung it off and pulled both doors open.

The puppets hung limply as we had left them.

"Stop, Ben. What are you doing?" Bird cried.

Jenny bumped him out of the way. "We have a major problem, Bird," she said. "Let Ben do what he has to do."

"But — but — but —" Bird sputtered.

I grabbed the princess puppet and tossed her to the floor. The sultan puppet hung right behind her. I grabbed it by the shoulders of its robe and tugged it from the cabinet.

I held it in front of me. "What did you do to me?" I screamed. "What did you do?"

The puppet stared up at me with its glassy eyes.

I let out a roar of anger. I started to shake it in both hands.

"Change me back! Change me back!" I shrieked. I was out of control. My chest throbbed with anger. The room was spinning all around me. I screamed in my tinny puppet voice at the top of my lungs and shook the puppet.

Its arms and legs flew wildly in the air. But its expression didn't change. And its glassy eyes kept their blank, lifeless gaze on me.

"Change me back! Change me back!" I cried.

No reaction.

I grabbed its head in one hand and its body in the other — and with a strong, wrenching move, I tried to rip the head off.

But the head remained attached to the shoulders. I lost my balance and fell into the wall.

"Change me back! Change me back!" I screamed.

I took the puppet by the legs and swung its head into the wall. Once. Twice. It made a loud *clunk* each time. But the puppet remained limp and lifeless.

Screaming in a rage, I held it in front of me and tried to rip its robe off. It wouldn't budge. I tugged at the turban. I couldn't pull it off the head. Again, I lowered my hand and tried to wrench the sultan's head off.

"Ben — stop! Stop!" Jenny's cry broke into my screams of rage.

Holding the puppet away from me, I struggled to catch my breath. My chest heaved up and down. My trembling puppet legs collapsed, and I dropped to the floor.

The puppet landed on its back. Its strings were tangled all around it. Its glassy eyes stared blankly up at me through the strings.

"I know what you did!" I choked out. "I know what you did to me. I know you're alive!"

I shook it again. I wanted to rip it to pieces. But I wasn't strong enough. I couldn't damage it in any way.

Finally, I tossed it to the floor and kicked it away from me.

Jenny and Bird dropped down beside me. Jenny put a hand on my trembling shoulders. "Take some deep breaths," she said. "Try to calm down, okay?"

"We'll get you to a doctor," Bird said.

My chest was still heaving up and down. I lowered my gaze to the floor. "Hey —" Something caught my eye. "What's that?" I pointed.

Jenny picked it up. A small white card. "It fell out of the sultan's robe when you shook him," she said.

"It looks like a business card," I said, my wooden lips clicking. "What does it say?"

Jenny raised it to her face and read it.

"Oh, wow," I murmured. "I don't believe it."

# 23

"What does it say?" Bird asked, still huddled beside me.

I read the card out loud:

*"Eduardo Caleb, Master Puppet Builder."*

There was an address under the name: *"150 Mulgrew Street."*

Bird stared at the card. "Mulgrew Street? Where's that?"

"I think it's in the old section of town," Jenny said. "Remember? I had an orthodontist somewhere over there?"

The card trembled in my hard puppet hand. "This *has* to be the guy," I said. "The guy who made these puppets and sold them to your dad."

"He can help you, Ben," Bird said. "He'll know what to do."

"Yes!" I cried, raising both hands above my head.

I saw my sister bite her bottom lip. And I saw a flash of fear in her eyes. "But . . . if this guy

Caleb made these puppets . . . maybe . . . maybe he's evil. Maybe he deliberately made them evil."

"He's my only chance," I said in my tinny voice, my mouth sliding up and down. "My only chance of being normal again. We have to go find him."

Jenny hesitated. "Shouldn't we wait for Mom and Dad? Or Bird's dad?"

"What if we wait, and it's too late?" I said. "My head feels more wooden every second. And my arms and feet are turning to wood, too. If we wait too long . . ."

"Let's go," Bird said. "We'll take these puppets with us. We'll give them back to this dude Caleb. We'll tell him we know the puppets are evil. We'll make him change you back, Ben. We can do it. I know we can."

Jenny and Bird stuffed the marionettes into a suitcase. Then we started for the bus stop two blocks away.

It was a warm morning. The sun was just climbing over the trees. A flock of blackbirds flew low overhead in a perfect V, cawing their heads off.

"Whoa. Are those birds bad luck?" I asked. "I don't need any more bad luck."

"Don't worry about them," Bird said. "Just concentrate on not being a puppet."

We walked across our neighbors' front lawns. I realized I was dragging my shoes through the grass. They suddenly seemed so heavy. Every few feet, my knees folded, and I had to struggle to stay on my feet.

We turned a corner, and bright sunlight made me blink. I raised one hand to shield my eyes — then gasped in horror.

"Oh, noooo — look!"

Jenny and Bird were walking a few feet ahead of me. They turned when they heard my cry.

I held my hand out toward them. "Look. I — I don't believe this. What am I going to *do*?"

Two small silver rings poked out of the skin on the back of my hand. I raised my other hand and squinted at it in the sunlight. Two little rings on that hand, too.

Bird's eyes were wide with horror. "You have them on the tops of your ears, too, Ben," he said in a whisper. "And there's one poking up from your hair."

"Wh-what are they?" I stammered, trembling in fright.

Jenny shook her head. "That's where the strings attach," she said.

# 24

I forced myself to breathe. I felt dizzy. Weak. My mind was whirring with nightmare thoughts.

"This means . . . I'm almost a puppet," I said, my mouth clicking up and down. I rubbed my aching forehead. It felt like hard wood.

"We've got to get you to Caleb," Jenny said. "Fast!"

Bird gripped the suitcase with the puppets inside in one hand. He put his other hand under my armpit. Jenny took my other arm. The two of them helped carry me to the bus stop.

My legs were too weak to walk. I kept staring at the little metal rings in my hands.

Luckily, we saw the bus turn the corner as soon as we reached the bus stop. Bird and Jenny helped me up the steps. We made our way to the middle of the bus. There were only two other passengers. Two men in work uniforms, one in the front, one in the back. They both kept nodding off to sleep.

Not too many people take the city bus on Saturday morning. Last year, I took the bus every Saturday morning to my guitar lessons downtown. But my guitar teacher moved away, and I haven't taken the bus since.

Funny how your brain keeps thinking of ordinary things, even when you're in major trouble. I watched the houses roll by outside the window and thought about my guitar lessons — even though I was about to become a marionette!

Bird and Jenny were silent. Jenny kept glancing down, then turning her eyes away. I knew what she was staring at. The little metal rings that had poked out of my skin.

The bus hit a bump, and all three of us jumped in our seats. My hands flew into the air, and my head shot back. I knew my head was turning to wood. It felt as if it weighed two tons.

The houses disappeared. The bus rumbled past some large gray factories. I took deep breaths and gazed out the window. I figured as long as I kept breathing, I'd still be human.

I thought about the three puppets jammed into the suitcase. Had they been alive once? Had they been real kids, too? Did a puppet stick its nose in their ears and turn them into puppets?

Or did this guy Eduardo Caleb do it to them?

Could they think? Could they see? My whole body shuddered. What if I ended up like them? Hanging in a closet or stuffed in a suitcase.

The bus squealed to a stop, and one of the workers climbed off. I gazed through the window. We were in a neighborhood of tall brick buildings. Small restaurants and rundown-looking shops lined the block.

A sign read FRIENDLY PAWN SHOP. The store next to it had a sign in the window CHECKS CASHED HERE. The next two shops had metal grates pulled down over their doors and windows. The grates were covered with graffiti.

"I think we're getting close," Jenny said. "Only a few blocks to go." She gripped Caleb's card between her fingers and kept glancing at the address.

We passed a vacant lot piled high with trash. And then some more stores that appeared to be empty and closed. The next block had a long, high fence stretching across it. Someone had scribbled with red paint FREDDY LIVES! In huge letters.

"Here we are. Let's get out," Jenny said.

She and Bird helped me to the front of the bus. The driver pulled to the curb and stopped. But he didn't open the door.

He studied us. He had tired blue eyes and a gray stubble of beard. "Are you sure you kids want to get out here?" he asked. "This is not a friendly neighborhood."

"We'll be careful," Jenny told him.

"We...have to meet someone," Bird explained.

The driver shrugged and pushed a button, and the doors slid apart.

"Thanks," Bird said. He helped me down to the sidewalk. Jenny joined us, and the bus pulled away.

I started to glance around — but a shrill scream made my breath catch in my throat.

I gasped as I heard a deafening crash. Metal shattering metal.

And a man's voice shrieked: "LOOK OUT!"

# 25

Jenny, Bird, and I dropped to our knees on the sidewalk. I covered my head with both hands and stayed frozen, not moving a muscle.

I heard the squeal of car tires. A man's voice rasped: "Stop — police."

I raised my head. I gazed at the open window across from us. A window blind flapped in the wind. And then I glimpsed the glare of the TV screen inside the window. Oh, wow.

The screams and crashes were coming from the TV.

I raised one hand and tapped Bird's shoulder. He was staring at the window, too. All three of us climbed to our feet.

"False alarm," Bird said.

"But the bus driver was right," I said. "This is a pretty creepy part of town."

Most of the stores on the street were closed and abandoned. Broken window glass crunched under our shoes as we started to walk. I heard a police siren in the distance. A door slammed. A bunch of teenagers came around the corner, running fast. They darted into the street, laughing and shoving each other.

"Keep close together," Jenny said. "This place is creeping me out."

We had no choice. We *had* to keep close together. Jenny and Bird had to half-carry me. My legs were too limp to hold me up.

"That's Mulgrew Street up there," Jenny said, pointing. "Now we just have to find the right number."

As we turned the corner, something caught my eye. "Whoa." I stopped and glanced back. I saw a flash of color disappear around the side of an apartment building.

"Ben — what's wrong?" Jenny asked.

"I think someone is following us," I said.

They turned and stared. "No one there," Bird said.

"I think they hid behind that building," I said.

"But who would follow us here?" Jenny asked.

I shut my eyes, trying to picture again what I'd seen. "I think it was Anna and Maria."

"That's too crazy," Jenny said.

"You're right," I agreed. "It's my eyes. They're becoming puppet eyes. I'm seeing weird things."

"We've got to hurry," Jenny said. "Your voice

is so tiny, I can barely hear you." She turned to Bird. "Look for street numbers. I know we're close. The number is one fifty."

I twisted my heavy head and looked behind us again. Was someone following us? I didn't see anyone.

"There it is," Bird said, pointing to a low brown building across the street. "One fifty Mulgrew Street."

We waited for two girls on bikes to go past. Then we crossed.

Jenny's eyes went wide with alarm. "The building is all boarded up," she said.

The doors and windows were covered with sheets of plywood. The shingles beside the front window were cracked and tilting toward the sidewalk.

We stepped over some crushed-up soda cans and other garbage to get closer. "There's a sign on the door," I said. "Can you read it?"

Bird darted closer and read the sign out loud: KEEP OUT. THIS BUILDING IS CONDEMNED.

# 26

"I don't believe it," I said, sighing. "We came all this way . . ."

We stared at the sign as if we could make it change its message. We stood there in silence for a long moment.

Clouds rolled over the morning sun, and a shadow fell over the street. The air suddenly carried a chill.

"What are we going to do?" I asked in a tiny voice. I squinted at the boarded-up windows on the front of the building. "I need help. Fast. Or else . . ." I couldn't finish my sentence.

Jenny tugged my arm. "We have to take you to Dr. Ackerman."

"But it's Saturday morning," Bird said, frowning. "He won't be in his office."

My mouth clicked up and down. "Besides, what can a doctor do? Look at me!" I raised both hands, with the tiny metal rings on the backs. "Is he going to give me anti-puppet medicine?"

They both stared at me openmouthed. A tear rolled down Jenny's cheek. "We have to find Mom and Dad. They —"

She stopped as a tall man strode up to us. He had a stained gray cap pulled over his head and wore baggy khakis torn at the knees. His eyes were as gray as his hat, and he had a stubble of white beard on his cheeks.

Too late to run. He had us backed against the building wall. My heart started to pound as he eyed us one by one.

"You looking for Caleb?" he said finally. His voice was hoarse, scratchy.

I nodded. "Yeah. We —"

"He moved away," the man said. The strange gray eyes locked on me. "Caleb moved. I don't know where he went. There's no one in there now."

He stuck a grimy hand out. "Do you have change for the bus? I'm trying to get home to Toledo."

"No. Sorry," I said. "We only have bus passes."

He nodded, scratching the stubble on his face. Then he turned and strode on down the street.

The sun came back and the buildings appeared to light up. But nothing could brighten my mood. I sighed again. "All this way for nothing," I murmured. My knees started to fold.

Jenny held me up by the arm. "We have to find the bus stop to go back," she said.

We peered across the street. A garbage truck rumbled past slowly. It left a sour aroma behind it.

"We have to cross Mulgrew," Bird said. "Is that a bus stop sign over there?" He pointed.

We took a few steps. Then I held back. "Hey — wait," I said.

"What's wrong?" Jenny asked.

"I think I saw someone," I said. I squinted at the boarded-up window beside the building entrance. "In that window. I saw a face."

"Probably just a reflection," Bird said. "The sunlight —"

"No." I pulled free from their hands. "I definitely saw someone looking out at us from that window. Maybe that guy was wrong. Maybe Caleb is still in there."

I didn't hesitate. I staggered to the door, forcing my rubbery legs to carry me. "We have to see if it's him," I said. "He's my only chance."

I raised my hand to the boarded-up door and knocked as hard as I could.

I listened hard. I couldn't hear any footsteps inside the building. I could still hear the rumbling of the garbage truck as it made its way down the block.

I knocked again. Bird stepped up beside me and pounded the door with both hands.

We waited.

Nothing happened.

"Please!" I shouted. "Please open the door! Please!" I totally lost it. I began to pound the door with both fists. "Please! I need help! Please!"

I pounded and pounded. I beat the door until my puppet hands throbbed with pain.

Silence. No one answered.

I turned to Jenny and Bird. "Say good-bye," I whispered. "I'm going to be a puppet now."

# 27

"No!" Jenny cried. "Don't give up. Maybe there's a back door."

"Right. A back door," Bird repeated. It was a desperate idea, but that's exactly what we were — desperate.

We made our way around the side of the building. We found ourselves in a narrow alley filled with trash. A cat yowled. The cry sounded like a human calling for help. Another cat joined in.

I stumbled over a pile of wet garbage and fell onto my stomach. Bird and Jenny pulled me up. The smell back here was totally sickening.

"I . . . I don't think we should be back here," Bird stammered.

I brushed sticky garbage off the front of my shirt.

"Look," Jenny said, pulling me forward. "Maybe that's the back door."

I raised my eyes and saw a narrow black door, the glass broken in the window. We made our way around an overturned trash can. Cats yowled all around, but I couldn't see them.

We stepped up to the door. I peered through the broken window. Nothing but darkness on the other side.

"Come on," I said. I grabbed the rusted doorknob and pushed hard. The door groaned, then slid open.

Bird held back. "Are we really going in here?"

I turned to him. My puppet eyes slid from side to side. "Do we have a choice?"

We found ourselves in a long, dark hallway. The only light came from sunlight through the broken window.

Our shoes scraped over the stone floor, which was covered in about an inch of dust. We passed open doorways with dark, empty rooms behind them.

"There's no one here," Bird whispered. "We seriously have to leave."

The hall turned and we followed it to the end. "Anyone home?" Jenny called. Her voice echoed as if we were in a deep tunnel. "Anyone home? Can anyone hear us?" she cried.

We stepped into a large, dimly lit room. Sunlight washed in through dust-caked windows along the top of the wall.

"I can't see a thing," I said, blinking hard.

"This place is too creepy," Bird said. "Let's go."

"I'm going to give it one more try," Jenny said. She cupped her hands around her mouth and shouted. "Can anyone hear us? Is anyone in this building?"

All three of us gasped as bright ceiling lights suddenly flashed on. And we stared at a wall of human faces.

# 28

The faces stared down at us, eyes glassy and blank. The mouths were turned up in red-lipped smiles.

My eyes shifted from face to face. They didn't move. They didn't blink. They stared down at us with the ugly grins on their shiny faces. It took me so long to realize they weren't human faces.

The three of us were staring at a wall of wooden puppet heads.

"Are you admiring my work?" a voice said behind us.

A startled cry escaped my throat. I spun around. And gazed at a smiling man in denim overalls and a red plaid shirt. He was short and a bit chubby, with a round red face and flashing blue eyes. He was bald except for a fringe of white hair above his ears. His smooth head appeared to shine under the bright lights.

"Welcome," he said softly. "How did you get in? The back door?"

I nodded. "Sorry if we —"

He raised a hand to silence me. "You must be clever kids not to be fooled by my *Condemned* sign or boarded-up windows. You see, I don't like visitors to interrupt me in my work."

"Are you Eduardo Caleb?" Jenny asked, huddling close to me.

He nodded. "Yes, I am. And as you can see, I am a puppet-maker." He motioned to the wall of heads.

"We have your card," Bird said, his voice cracking. "We came here because Ben —"

"I need help," I blurted out. "They brought me here because I'm in trouble." I raised both hands. "Do you see what's happening to me?"

Caleb's eyes bulged as he studied me. "Oh, how horrible. You have been infected, Ben."

My mouth clicked open. "Infected?"

"The puppet cells grow quickly," he said. He stepped forward and gently picked up my hand. He studied it for a long moment. He squeezed the little metal rings poking out of my skin. "I'd say you have half an hour at most."

"B-but . . . can you help me?" I stammered.

He nodded, still holding on to my hand. "I'm the only one in the world who can help you, young man." He lowered his eyes. His smile was almost shy. "It's good you found me in time. I'll take good care of you, I promise."

Suddenly, he turned to Bird. "What do you have in that suitcase?"

"Marionettes," Bird answered. He set the suitcase on the floor and bent to open it. "Three of them. I think they're yours."

Caleb's blue eyes flashed wide with surprise when Bird pulled out the princess and the sultan. He frowned and shook his head. "Failures," he muttered.

He picked up the knight puppet from the suitcase and raised it in front of him. "I never should have sold these puppets. They weren't made right. And I knew they would infect others."

He frowned. "I've been trying to find them. For years, I've been trying to track them down, hoping I could get to them before they spread their evil."

"It was the sultan," I said, my wooden lips clicking. "He infected me. He poked his nose into my ear and — and —"

"Stay calm," Caleb said softly. "You are here now, son. I'll make sure you are right again."

He took the three puppets and tossed them onto the floor. They lay in a tangle of arms, legs, and strings. "Don't worry. I'll make sure these three failures never harm anyone again."

He patted me gently on the shoulder. "Look what they've done to you. It isn't right. I am so sorry this happened. I take full responsibility."

I stared up at him, into his warm blue eyes. "Can you really turn me back to normal?" My shrill puppet voice came from somewhere inside my chest. My glassy eyes slid from side to side.

"Of course," he said. "It won't take long at all." One hand on my shoulder, he started to guide me from the room. "I'm going to put you under my electron dome," he said. "You'll be the old Ben in less than five minutes. I promise."

Caleb turned to Bird and Jenny. "Don't just stand there. Come along with us. You want to watch, don't you?"

They both started to follow us.

My heart was pounding. I told myself to be calm, that I was in good hands. I'd be okay again soon. But my head spun and the floor tilted from side to side.

At the doorway, I glanced back. My eyes stopped on the tangle of puppets on the floor. *Were they moving?*

I blinked. Yes. All three of them.

I stared hard till I realized what they were doing. They were shaking their heads no.

# 29

Caleb saw that I was staring at the three puppets. "They are so evil," he whispered. "I am ashamed that I made them. They were a terrible mistake."

"But why are they shaking their heads?" Bird asked. He saw them, too. "Are they trying to tell us something?"

"They are evil troublemakers, pure and simple," Caleb replied. "I'm so glad you brought them back to me. I can make sure they never harm anyone again."

"Whoa. Hold on a minute. Were they real kids?" Jenny asked. "Were they real kids who changed into puppets the way Ben is changing?"

"No. Of course not," Caleb said. "I'm just a puppet-maker. That's all I do." He turned to me. "Come. Hurry. I'll answer all your questions later. We haven't much time."

He led us down another hallway. The lights were bright here. I heard classical music playing in a room we passed. The next room appeared to be a workshop. A stack of dark lumber stood beside a long workbench.

"We have to get you under the dome right away, Ben," Caleb said. "The longer we wait, the longer it will take to stop the infection. Once your hands and feet harden to wood . . ." His voice trailed off.

A chill of fear rolled down my back. "But you can do it, right?" I said. "You said you can turn me back into myself."

He nodded. "I can do it. I promise. I can do it."

He led us into a large, brightly lit room. It appeared to be a science lab. I saw a row of laptop computers on a table, as well as a lot of electrical equipment, humming and beeping.

Caleb led us to a long metal table in the center of the lab.

"It looks like an operating table," Bird said. "Like in those TV shows about hospitals."

Caleb smiled. He rubbed his smooth red cheeks. "I won't be doing any operating, my friends. I'm not a doctor." He pointed up to the high ceiling. "That's the dome up there."

A large green dome hung high over the table. It looked like the lid to my mom's roasting pan, the one she cooks the Thanksgiving turkey in.

*I'm going to be the turkey*, I thought with a shudder.

"It's all very simple," Caleb said to me. "You

lie down on the table. I'll get you a pillow for your head so you are comfortable. Then I'll lower the dome over you and turn on the electrons. It shouldn't take long at all."

"And when you lift the dome —?" I started.

"You'll know right away that you are okay. You'll feel perfectly normal again."

I turned to Jenny and Bird. They stood tensely at the wall. Both had their eyes on the humming, beeping electronic equipment.

"Wish me luck," I said.

"You don't need luck, Ben," Caleb said softly. "You're in good hands. Come on. Let's go."

He helped lift me onto the metal table. It felt surprisingly warm. I stretched out on my back, my arms and legs limp. Once again, I stared at the rings where puppet strings would be attached.

Caleb slid a pillow under my head. He chuckled. "Relax, fella. Close your eyes. Take a rest."

I pressed my head against the pillow. I gazed up at the green dome suspended from the ceiling. Then I blinked in surprise as Caleb strapped a tight belt over my waist.

"Relax," he repeated.

He pulled wire cuffs from the sides of the table and cuffed my hands down at my sides.

"Hey —!" I cried out. "What are you doing?"

"It's no problem, Ben," he said. "I need to keep you very still." He leaned over me and locked his blue eyes on mine. "I need you to trust me. Do you trust me?"

I hesitated. "Yes," I said finally. "But I didn't think you were going to strap me down."

He took one of my hands and tapped both sides. "Your skin is getting pretty hard. But I think we're still in time."

He turned and crossed to the table of laptops. He sat down in front of one of them and began tapping on the keyboard.

I stared straight up and watched as the huge dome slowly lowered itself over the table.

I tried to relax, as he had instructed. But as the shadow of the dome slid over me, I couldn't keep the frightening questions from repeating over and over in my mind:

*Is he really going to help me? Have I made a horrible mistake?*

The dome clanged as it touched the table. A heavy darkness fell over me. And suddenly I was gasping for breath.

"Stop!" I shouted. "Stop now! I can't breathe!"

# 30

I tugged at the cuffs that held my hands down. My heart leaped around in my chest. My whole body shuddered. *I've got to get out of here.*

"Relax, Ben." Caleb's voice came through a tiny speaker in the metal dome. "Shut your eyes and breathe normally."

I forced my panic down. I tried to follow his instructions. The metal dome started to vibrate. A loud hum rose up and down. It sounded like a swarm of bees.

I took a deep breath and held it.

"You're doing fine, Ben," Caleb said in his soft, gentle voice. "Keep breathing slowly. It's going to vibrate a little, but it won't get too rough."

I breathed in. Breathed out. My heart was still hopping about like a frog in my chest. My hands strained against the cuffs.

The vibrations grew stronger. The hum became

a buzzing drone, rising and falling like a police siren.

"Doing fine. Doing fine," Caleb said.

My skin started to tingle. The vibrations were inside me now. I could feel my whole body vibrating.

A rattling sound made me want to cover my ears. But, of course, my hands were tied down. I tried to test my legs. Were they back to normal? Could I raise them?

The dome was too low to move them very far.

A high, shrill screech made me cry out. My whole body twisted in shock.

"No problem, Ben." Caleb's voice came softly through the little speaker. "Don't be alarmed. You're doing well. Just another minute."

Another screech. Like metal scraping against metal.

It made me grit my teeth. I clamped my eyes shut. I tightened my hands into fists.

"You're doing well, Ben." Caleb never raised his voice. He stayed calm and quiet. "Relax. Relax. No need to be tense. That's just the electrons adjusting. You're almost done."

And then, the hum stopped. The dome stopped vibrating.

I opened my eyes. I slowly unclenched my fists.

"You did very well, Ben," Caleb said. "I'm going to raise the dome now."

The big dome made a creaking sound as it started to lift off the table. I gazed up at it, watching it glide back up to its place under the ceiling.

Then I raised my head, blinking in the bright light. Bird and Jenny hadn't moved from the wall.

I took a deep breath. "Am I okay?" I asked in a trembling voice. "Am I back to normal?"

# 31

Caleb sat at his laptop, hunched over the keyboard, his face frozen in the glare of the screen. Bird and Jenny hesitated. Then they left their spots at the wall and ran over to me at the table.

"Am I okay?" I repeated. "Do I look like myself again?"

They leaned over the table and studied me. Jenny lifted my hand and ran her fingers over the front and back of it. "No metal rings in your skin," she reported.

Bird tapped my forehead with his fist. "Normal," he said. "Skin, not wood."

I raised my legs. Kicked my feet up and down. "Hey — I feel like myself!" I cried. "Yaaaay!"

"I keep my promises," Caleb said, still at the computer table. "I told you you'd be normal again, and you are."

"I . . . I can't thank you enough," I stammered. "I'm *me* again. I'm not going to spend the rest of my life as a puppet hanging in someone's closet. I'm so happy! Can I get up now?"

"Not quite yet," Caleb said.

A stab of fear chilled the back of my neck. "Huh? Why not?"

"I haven't finished with you yet," Caleb replied. He squeezed my shoulder. "Now that I've cleaned the *bad* puppet out of you, I'm going to turn you into the greatest puppet anyone has ever seen!"

"But — but —" I sputtered, straining at the belt that held me down. "No — wait! Please! What are you doing? What do you *mean*?"

I gazed up and saw the big green dome sliding down again.

# 32

"WAIT!" I screamed. "STOP! I don't understand. What are you doing?"

"Those three puppets on the floor out there were of poor quality," Caleb explained. "Inferior. Beneath my talents. You were about to become an inferior puppet, too. But I cleaned you. I got rid of the puppet infection."

"And now —?"

"I cured you so I could turn you into a better puppet!" Caleb exclaimed. "You will be amazing! You will be a winner, Ben. You will be famous. The world's most famous puppet!"

I watched the dome slowly lowering to the table. "No! Please —" I begged. "Please!" I struggled to pull myself up. But my waist and hands were tightly fastened.

"Let him go!" Jenny screamed. "You can't do this!"

"Out of my way!" Caleb cried. He shoved

Jenny and Bird aside and darted toward his computer table.

But he didn't get there.

I turned my head when I heard a clattering at the door. The dome hung a few feet above the table. I raised my head — and saw the three puppets stagger into the room. They moved quickly to surround the startled Caleb.

The knight raised his sword. The princess tackled Caleb around the knees. The sultan leaped onto Caleb, covering his head with his long purple robe.

"Revenge!" the sultan screamed in a deep, booming voice. "Revenge for all you did to us!"

"Go away! Get out of my way!" Caleb screeched, thrashing his arms at them. "You are inferior! Get away from me! You are inferior!"

The puppets fell upon him, tangling him in their costumes and their strings.

Jenny and Bird wasted no time. They unfastened the belt over my chest and uncuffed my hands. Bird grabbed my hand and hoisted me down from the table. "Let's go!"

"Come back!" Caleb wailed, still struggling to untangle himself from the three puppets. "Ben, I can make you great! I can make you famous!"

I took a deep breath and followed Bird and Jenny out of the lab. We were running full speed. Our shoes slapped the dusty floor as we bolted back down the long halls.

Did I glimpse someone in a doorway? Was someone else in the building? I didn't stop to find out.

We ran out into the alley and kept running. The sunlight felt so good on my face. My *human* face.

We waved down the bus and jumped onboard. Great timing.

My heart was still racing as we took seats in the back. "What were we thinking?" I said. "How could we have been that crazy just to win five hundred dollars in a dumb school variety show?"

"You're right," Bird said. "That was crazy. We'll have more fun. We can sit in the audience and boo everyone!"

As we rode away, we thought it was the end of the puppet people. But Caleb had one more surprise for us. . . .

# 33

On the afternoon of the variety show, Bird, Jenny, and I sat in the third row of the auditorium, ready to boo everyone who performed. Of course, I planned to save my loudest boos for Anna and Maria.

Teddy Swanson came onstage first. He did a pretty good yodeling song. The audience started clapping along. Teddy could really yodel.

But halfway through, something got stuck in his throat, and Teddy had to run offstage to get a drink of water. When he came back, his voice kept cracking and he couldn't yodel at all. He trudged offstage, shaking his head.

Everyone clapped, but it was sarcastic clapping.

"Be nice, everyone," Mrs. O'Neal warned. She introduced the Barry sisters, Courtney and Jessica. They played kazoos. Totally embarrassing.

"Please. Shoot me now," I whispered to Jenny.

She raised a finger to her lips. "Give them a break."

"But Courtney can't even remember the tune," I whispered.

"It's harder than it looks," Jenny replied.

Bird started bopping in his seat and clapping along. But he was just being funny.

Vee Cheng came onstage next and played a solo clarinet version of an old Elton John song. After a minute or two, she messed up. She lowered her clarinet and turned to Mrs. O'Neal. "Can I start over?"

"Just keep going, Vee," Mrs. O'Neal said cheerily. "We're all enjoying it."

Vee kept going. And she played beautifully. We didn't boo her. She was too good.

"And now we have a very unusual puppet act," Mrs. O'Neal announced.

Puppets? I sat forward in my seat and stared at the stage.

Two tall puppeteers wearing red ski masks over their faces strode to the front of the curtain. I studied them for a while. I didn't recognize them.

Then my eyes lowered to the marionettes they held — and I gasped in shock.

The puppets were life-sized. And so totally real looking.

I was so startled, it took me a while to recognize them. The puppets were Anna and Maria!

The two masked puppeteers were operating Anna and Maria puppets. They made the two girls spin around and do a wild dance.

I couldn't breathe. I couldn't move. I knew I was watching *living puppet people.*

I turned to Jenny. Her eyes were also bulging in shock.

"Jenny," I whispered. "Anna and Maria — they *did* follow us to Caleb's lab. Look at them. Look at them!"

I squeezed her arm. I shook my head in disbelief.

"Oh, wow. Wow. They followed us to Caleb's," Jenny said. "And Caleb did it! He turned them into puppets!"

And now everyone recognized the two girls, and the audience began going nuts. The whole auditorium erupted in cheers and shouts and wild applause.

The two girl-puppets whirled across the stage. Howls and shrieks rang out from the kids watching and echoed off the auditorium walls. It had to be the most amazing, most *awesome* thing anyone had ever seen.

Anna and Maria were now puppets, and beneath their strings, they glided and slid and bowed and stepped in a beautiful, graceful dance.

I turned to Jenny and Bird. I had to shout over the screams and cheers of the crowd. "Do you believe it?" I cried. "They win again!"

## He'll come when you call!

# HERE COMES THE SHAGGEDY

## Here's a sneak peek!

# 1

The swamp at night makes trickling sounds, gurgling, popping. The river water is alive, and the sand shifts and moves as if it's restless. The chitter and whistle of insects never stops. Birds flap in the low, bent trees, and red-eyed bats flutter low, dipping into the water for a fast drink, then soaring to meet the darkness.

The eerie sounds made Becka Munroe's skin tingle. She sat alert in the slender rowboat, every muscle in her body tensed and tight. She kept her eyes on the dark shore line. Her hands on the oars felt cold and wet.

"Donny, you're crazy," she said, her voice muffled in the steamy night air. "I don't like this. We shouldn't be here."

"They won't miss their stupid rowboat," her boyfriend Donny Albert said. His oars splashed water, then hit sand. The river was shallow enough here for their boat to get stuck. "We'll leave it for them up shore."

"I'm not talking about stealing this boat," Becka said, fighting the shivers that rolled down her back despite the heat of the night. "Why are we here? Why are we on the river at night in this frightening swamp? I . . . I can't see a thing. There isn't even a moon."

Donny snickered. "For thrills," he said. "Life is so boring, Becka. Tenth grade is so boring. Go to school. Do your homework. Sleep and go to school again. We have to do something crazy. Something exciting."

Becka sighed. "I can't believe I agreed to come out here at night. Why did I do it?"

She could see his grin even in the dim light. "Because you're crazy about me?"

"Just plain crazy," she muttered.

Something splashed up from the water and thumped the side of the boat. "Did you hear that?" Becka cried. "What was it? A frog?"

"Snake maybe," Donny said. "The river is crawling with them. Some are a mile long."

"Shut up!" Becka snapped. She had a sudden urge to take an oar and swing it at Donny's head. "You're not funny. It's scary enough out here without you trying to scare me more."

He laughed. "You're too easy to scare. It's not much of a challenge. I don't think —"

He didn't finish his sentence. His mouth remained open and his dark eyes bulged. He was staring past Becka. His chin began to quiver and a low moan escaped his throat. He raised a finger and pointed.

Becka heard the splash of water behind her. And the heavy *slap* of footsteps on wet sand. "Donny — what —?" she uttered. Then she turned and saw the huge creature.

It took her eyes a few seconds to focus. At first, she thought she was staring at a tall swamp bush, some kind of piney shrub looming up from the sandy bottom.

But as soon as she realized it was moving in the water, taking long, wet, splashing strides . . . she knew it was alive. Knew it was a terrifying creature.

"Row! Hurry! Row!" Donny's scream came out high and shrill. He bent over the oars and began to pull frantically. She could hear his wheezing breaths. But they were quickly drowned out by the grunts of the swamp monster that staggered toward them and its thudding wet footsteps.

The creature stood at least ten feet tall. It was shaped like a human but covered in dark fur like a bear. Chunks of wet sand fell off its fur as it staggered forward. And it raised curled claws and uttered an angry howl of attack.

"Oh, help. Oh, help." One oar slipped out of Becka's hand. She grabbed at it and caught it before it dropped into the water. She didn't even hear her muttered cries. She leaned forward and began to row as hard as she could.

"Row faster!" Donny cried. "Faster! We can get away. It's slow. We can get —"

A hard jolt shook them both. Their bodies snapped forward, then back. The oars flew from Donny's hands.

Becka knew at once what had happened. The boat had hit a sand bar.

The swamp creature uttered another animal cry, like a bleating elephant. Water splashed high as it leaned forward, brought its clawed paws down, preparing to grab them.

His oars in the water, Donny rocked the boat from side to side. Becka desperately dug her oars into the sand, pulling . . . pulling.

Its prow stuck deep in the sloping sand hill, the boat didn't move. The two teenagers sat helpless as the grunting, howling creature advanced.

And as it loomed over them, spreading its arms, gnashing its pointed teeth, their final screams echoed off the bent trees, sending bats fluttering to the sky.

"What are you doing? Turn that off!"

Kelli Anderson jumped at the sound of her father's voice.

She watched him stride across the den, grab the remote, and click off the TV. He turned and squinted through his black-framed eyeglasses at Kelli and her brother Shawn. They sat on the edges of the long black leather couch, a bowl of nacho chips between them.

Kelli crossed her arms in front of her and glared at him. "Why did you turn it off at the good part?" she demanded.

"Why were you watching that movie?" he asked. "*Swamp Beast III*?"

Shawn had his hands clasped tightly in his lap. His dark eyes were wide, his expression frightened. "Kelli wanted to show me where you're making us move to," he whispered.

Their dad shook his head. "By watching a horror movie?" He took off his glasses and rubbed the top of his nose. He did that a lot. It either meant he was thinking hard or he was trying to control his temper.

"Kelli, you're twelve," he said. "You're the older sister. You should know better."

"But, Dad —" Kelli started.

He raised a hand. "Silence. You know your brother is afraid of scary movies. You know Shawn has nightmares. How could you be so thoughtless?"

Kelli shrugged. "I . . . didn't think it would be that scary."

Of course that was a lame reply, but it was the best she could do. Kelli knew the truth. She really *did* want to scare Shawn. If he was seriously scared, maybe their dad wouldn't drag them away from New York City to a Florida swamp.

Shawn did that thing with his shoulders that he always did when he was feeling tense or scared. He kind of rolled them so that it looked like he was shivering. "Dad . . . ?" he started in a tiny voice. "Are there really swamp monsters where we are moving?"

Kelli groaned.

Their dad's cheeks reddened. He was totally bald, and when he got angry, the top of his head turned red, too. Kelli always thought he looked like a light bulb lighting up. A light bulb with glasses.

"Of *course* there aren't any swamp monsters," he told Shawn. He turned to Kelli. "Look how you scared Shawn. You should apologize to him."

Kelli tried to recite the multiplication table to calm down. But she was terrible with numbers. She didn't get past 2 times 2. "Sorry, Shawn," she finally muttered. "Sorry you got scared by a dumb movie."

"That's not much of an apology," her dad said. "*You* get scared sometimes, don't you, Kelli?"

"No," she answered. "I don't. Never."

Shawn suddenly shot his head forward and screamed, "BOO!" practically in Kelli's ear. He laughed. "Made you jump."

"Did not," Kelli said. "You can't scare me, wimpo."

"Hey, what have we said about calling names?" their dad demanded. He didn't wait for an answer. "Listen, you two. Living next to Deep Hole Swamp is going to be the most exciting year of your lives."

"Maybe *too* exciting," Kelli said. She tossed back her black hair. She knew she was about to cause trouble. About to frighten Shawn and annoy her father even more. But she didn't really care. *Whatever works*, she thought. *Whatever it takes to keep me in New York City with my friends.*

Her dad took the bait. "What do you mean by that, Kelli?"

"I went online," she said. "I read stuff about Deep Hole Swamp. A lot of people say there are monsters living in the swamp. Just like in *Swamp Beast III*."

"Really?" Shawn asked in a tiny voice. He did his shoulder thing again.

"No. Not really," their father said, frowning at Kelli. "You know there's a lot of bad information online. You don't trust everything you read — do you?"

Kelli's dark eyes challenged her father. "Some things are true."

"Well, monster stories aren't true," he said. "I'm a scientist, remember?"

Kelli rolled her eyes. "We know. We know. Dr. Andersen. You're a marine biologist. You remind us every day."

Her dad gritted his teeth. Kelli knew she was making him angry. But she didn't care. She really didn't want to move to a swamp in Florida for a year.

After their parents divorced, their mom moved to Seattle. Kelli didn't want to live there, either. She only wanted to live in New York. Now she was going to have to split her time between TWO places she hated.

She saw Shawn, skinny, pale Shawn, sitting on the edge of the couch, trembling. She felt bad that she had to scare him. But what choice did she have?

## About the Author

R.L. Stine's books are read all over the world. So far, his books have sold more than 300 million copies, making him one of the most popular children's authors in history. Besides Goosebumps, R.L. Stine has written the teen series Fear Street and the funny series Rotten School, as well as the Mostly Ghostly series, The Nightmare Room series, and the two-book thriller *Dangerous Girls*. R.L. Stine lives in New York with his wife, Jane, and Minnie, his King Charles spaniel. You can learn more about him at www.RLStine.com.

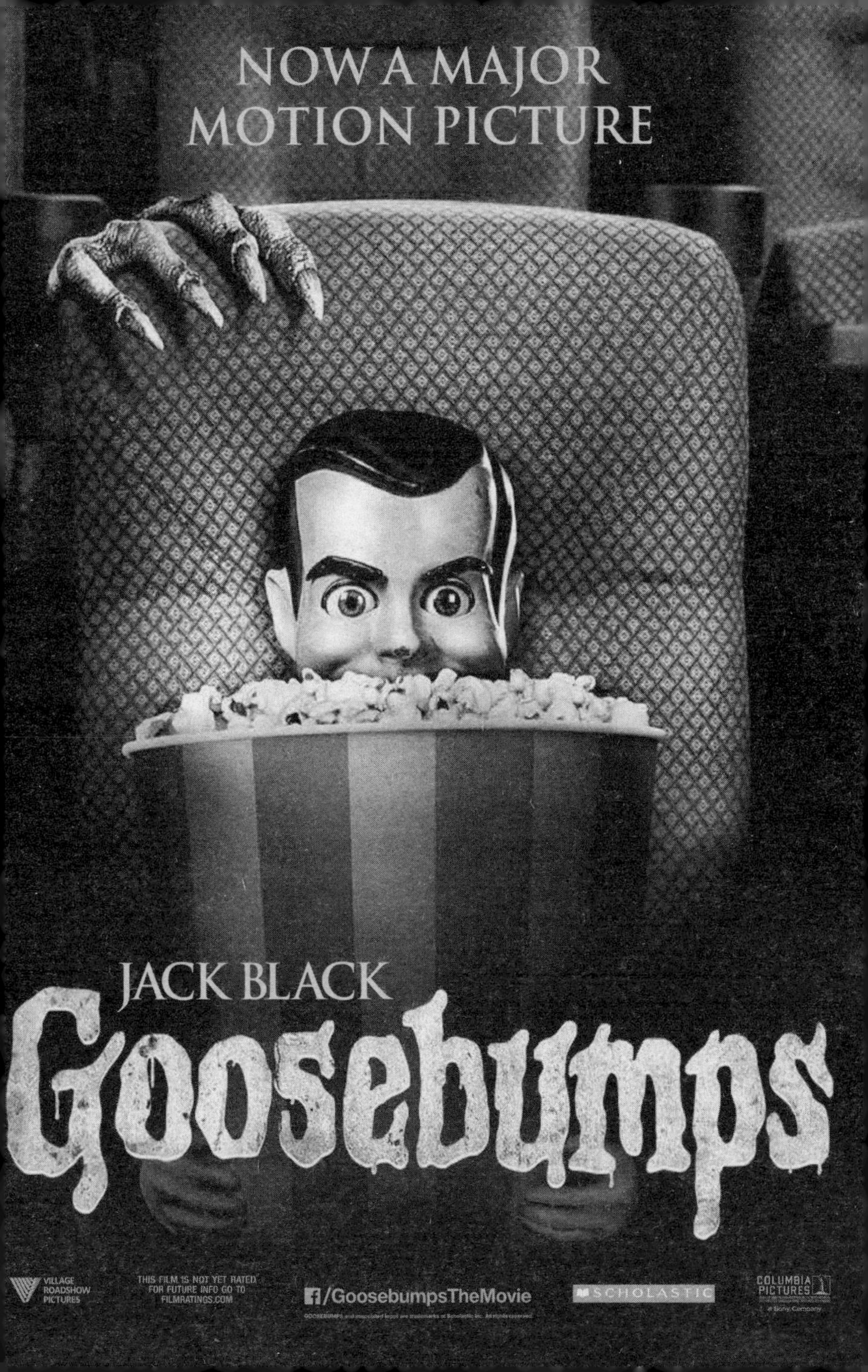
NOW A MAJOR
MOTION PICTURE
JACK BLACK
Goosebumps
VILLAGE ROADSHOW PICTURES
THIS FILM IS NOT YET RATED
FOR FUTURE INFO GO TO
FILMRATINGS.COM
/GoosebumpsTheMovie
SCHOLASTIC
COLUMBIA PICTURES
a Sony Company

# The Original Bone-Chilling Series

Goosebumps®

**—with Exclusive Author Interviews!**

NIGHT of the LIVING DUMMY
R.L. STINE

DEEP TROUBLE
R.L. STINE

MONSTER BLOOD
R.L. STINE

the HAUNTED MASK
R.L. STINE

ONE DAY at HORRORLAND
R.L. STINE

the CURSE of the MUMMY'S TOMB
R.L. STINE

BE CAREFUL WHAT YOU WISH FOR
R.L. STINE

SAY CHEESE and DIE!
R.L. STINE

the HORROR at CAMP JELLYJAM
R.L. STINE

HOW I GOT MY SHRUNKEN HEAD
R.L. STINE

Goosebumps
GHASTLY MISCHIEF AWAITS...
WWW.SCHOLASTIC.COM/GOOSEBUMPS
EXPLORE EVERY BOOK!
GET GHOUL-YARD GOSSIP!
PLAY THRILLING GAMES!
SAMPLE SPOOKY AUDIOBOOKS!
JOIN THE FAN FORUM!
WATCH MONSTROUS VIDEOS!

# Catch the
# MOST WANTED
# Goosebumps® villains
# UNDEAD OR ALIVE!